seemed to grow larger than they were already.

Then they seemed to blaze at the Duke.

"I swear before God and on my father's grave," she said, "that every word I have told you is the truth!"

She glared at the Duke as she went on:

"If the Princess means . . . more to you than the . . . lives of your own countrymen, then there is . . . nothing I can do . . . about it!"

Before the Duke could stop her she disappeared out of the room.

She heard him call out "Solita!" but as he did so she ran down the empty corridor to her own bed-room . . .

A Camfield Novel of Love
by Barbara Cartland

———

"Barbara Cartland's novels are all distinguished by their intelligence, good sense, and good nature . . ."
— **ROMANTIC TIMES**

"Who could give better advice on how to keep your romance going strong than the world's most famous romance novel-ist, Barbara Cartland?"
— **THE STAR**

"You are making this up!" the Duke exclaimed.

His anger took Solita by surprise and her eyes

Dearest Reader,

Camfield Novels of Love mark a very exciting era of my books with Jove. They have already published nearly two hundred of my titles since they became my first publisher in America, and now all my original paperback romances in the future will be published exclusively by them.

As you already know, Camfield Place in Hertfordshire is my home, which originally existed in 1275, but was rebuilt in 1867 by the grandfather of Beatrix Potter.

It was here in this lovely house, with the best view in the county, that she wrote *The Tale of Peter Rabbit*. Mr. McGregor's garden is exactly as she described it. The door in the wall that the fat little rabbit could not squeeze underneath and the goldfish pool where the white cat sat twitching its tail are still there.

I had Camfield Place blessed when I came here in 1950 and was so happy with my husband until he died, and now with my children and grandchildren, that I know the atmosphere is filled with love and we have all been very lucky.

It is easy here to write of love and I know you will enjoy the Camfield Novels of Love. Their plots are definitely exciting and the covers very romantic. They come to you, like all my books, with love.

Bless you,

Barbara Cartland

CAMFIELD NOVELS OF LOVE

by Barbara Cartland

THE POOR GOVERNESS
WINGED VICTORY
LUCKY IN LOVE
LOVE AND THE MARQUIS
A MIRACLE IN MUSIC
LIGHT OF THE GODS
BRIDE TO A BRIGAND
LOVE COMES WEST
A WITCH'S SPELL
SECRETS
THE STORMS OF LOVE
MOONLIGHT ON THE
    SPHINX
WHITE LILAC
REVENGE OF THE HEART
THE ISLAND OF LOVE
THERESA AND A TIGER
LOVE IS HEAVEN
MIRACLE FOR A MADONNA
A VERY UNUSUAL WIFE
THE PERIL AND THE
    PRINCE
ALONE AND AFRAID
TEMPTATION OF A
    TEACHER
ROYAL PUNISHMENT

THE DEVILISH DECEPTION
PARADISE FOUND
LOVE IS A GAMBLE
A VICTORY FOR LOVE
LOOK WITH LOVE
NEVER FORGET LOVE
HELGA IN HIDING
SAFE AT LAST
HAUNTED
CROWNED WITH LOVE
ESCAPE
THE DEVIL DEFEATED
THE SECRET OF THE
    MOSQUE
A DREAM IN SPAIN
THE LOVE TRAP
LISTEN TO LOVE
THE GOLDEN CAGE
LOVE CASTS OUT FEAR
A WORLD OF LOVE
DANCING ON A RAINBOW
LOVE JOINS THE CLANS
AN ANGEL RUNS AWAY
FORCED TO MARRY
BEWILDERED IN BERLIN

WANTED—A WEDDING
    RING
THE EARL ESCAPES
STARLIGHT OVER TUNIS
THE LOVE PUZZLE
LOVE AND KISSES
SAPPHIRES IN SIAM
A CARETAKER OF LOVE
SECRETS OF THE HEART
RIDING IN THE SKY
LOVERS IN LISBON
LOVE IS INVINCIBLE
THE GODDESS OF LOVE
AN ADVENTURE OF LOVE
THE HERB FOR HAPPINESS
ONLY A DREAM
SAVED BY LOVE
LITTLE TONGUES OF FIRE
A CHIEFTAIN FINDS LOVE
THE LOVELY LIAR
PERFUME OF THE GODS
A KNIGHT IN PARIS
REVENGE IS SWEET
THE PASSIONATE PRINCESS
SOLITA AND THE SPIES

Other books by Barbara Cartland

THE ADVENTURER
AGAIN THIS RAPTURE
BARBARA CARTLAND'S
    BOOK OF BEAUTY AND
    HEALTH
BLUE HEATHER
BROKEN BARRIERS
THE CAPTIVE HEART
THE COIN OF LOVE
THE COMPLACENT WIFE
COUNT THE STARS
DESIRE OF THE HEART
DESPERATE DEFIANCE
THE DREAM WITHIN
ELIZABETHAN LOVER
THE ENCHANTING EVIL
ESCAPE FROM PASSION
FOR ALL ETERNITY
A GOLDEN GONDOLA
A HAZARD OF HEARTS
A HEART IS BROKEN
THE HIDDEN HEART
THE HORIZONS OF LOVE
IN THE ARMS OF LOVE

THE IRRESISTIBLE BUCK
THE KISS OF PARIS
THE KISS OF THE DEVIL
A KISS OF SILK
THE KNAVE OF HEARTS
THE LEAPING FLAME
A LIGHT TO THE HEART
LIGHTS OF LOVE
THE LITTLE PRETENDER
LOST ENCHANTMENT
LOVE AT FORTY
LOVE FORBIDDEN
LOVE IN HIDING
LOVE IS THE ENEMY
LOVE ME FOREVER
LOVE TO THE RESCUE
LOVE UNDER FIRE
THE MAGIC OF HONEY
METTERNICH THE
    PASSIONATE DIPLOMAT
MONEY, MAGIC AND
    MARRIAGE
NO HEART IS FREE
THE ODIOUS DUKE

OPEN WINGS
A RAINBOW TO HEAVEN
THE RELUCTANT BRIDE
THE SCANDALOUS LIFE
    OF KING CAROL
THE SECRET FEAR
THE SMUGGLED
    HEART
A SONG OF LOVE
STARS IN MY HEART
STOLEN HALO
SWEET ENCHANTRESS
SWEET PUNISHMENT
THEFT OF A HEART
THE THIEF OF LOVE
THIS TIME IT'S LOVE
TOUCH A STAR
TOWARDS THE STARS
THE UNKNOWN HEART
WE DANCED ALL NIGHT
THE WINGS OF ECSTASY
THE WINGS OF LOVE
WINGS ON MY HEART
WOMAN, THE ENIGMA

A NEW CAMFIELD NOVEL OF LOVE BY

BARBARA CARTLAND

Solita and the Spies

J

JOVE BOOKS, NEW YORK

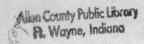
SOLITA AND THE SPIES

A Jove Book/published by arrangement with
the author

PRINTING HISTORY
Jove edition/July 1989

ISBN: 0-515-10058-7

Jove Books are published by The Berkley Publishing Group,
200 Madison Avenue, New York, New York 10016.
The name "JOVE" and the "J" logo
are trademarks belonging to Jove Publications, Inc.

PRINTED IN THE UNITED STATES OF AMERICA

10 9 8 7 6 5 4 3 2 1

Author's Note

THE British invented Submarine Cables and by the 1890s had encompassed their Empire with them.

Between 1870 and 1897 the Colonial Office Telegraph bill had risen from 800 pounds a year to about 8,000.

The net-work had its weaknesses, but it was an amazing speeding up of communications which is unparalleled in history.

The first routes to India were unsatisfactory, as they ran across hostile countries and were constantly interfered with.

In 1870 the British opened a Submarine Cable via Gibraltar, Malta, Alexandria, Suez, and Aden to Bombay—safely marked in red on the globe.

If any of these routes were cut, there was no Southern link from India. The only alternative route was the vulnerable line to Australia through Java.

All over the world Englishmen were at work, laying and maintaining these cables or operating "booster" stations along the line.

The centre station of the Overland Telegraph at Alice Springs was one of the loneliest places in the Empire.

It was a thousand miles South of Darwin and a

thousand miles North of Adelaide, the nearest towns.

Yet sometimes the sudden clatter of the Morse machine miraculously linked Alice Springs for a minute or two with Calcutta, Malta, and the Imperial Capital on the other side of the world.

All this vast expertise of ships and mails and cable stations made the British master of International movement.

Nobody else operated on such a scale and, as Kipling wrote in his poem called "The Deep Sea Cables":

> They have wakened the timeless Things; they
>   have killed their father Time;
> Joining hands in the gloom a league from the
>   last of the sun.
> Hush! Men talk today o'er the waste of the ul-
>   timate slime,
> And a new Word runs between: whispering,
>   "Let us be one!"

chapter one

1882

THE train came to a standstill and Solita, looking out, realised she had arrived at her destination.

Her trunk was with her in the same carriage because when she told the porter where she was going he had said:

"That be a 'Alt, Miss, an' the Guard's Van don't come up to t'platform."

She had not understood until she saw now that the Halt consisted of a very small building and a platform which was little more than the length of one carriage.

She stepped out and a porter who seemed somewhat old and decrepit pulled out her trunk.

As he did so, two smartly dressed footmen in a spectacular livery walked across the platform to the carriage next to hers.

She realised they were meeting somebody who had travelled in the same train as she had, but she was not particularly interested.

Instead, she said to the porter who was wheeling away her trunk in a truck:

"I would like a Hackney Carriage, please."

"Ye won't foind one 'ere," he replied.

Solita did not believe him until they were outside the Halt, then she saw only two vehicles there.

One was a very smart Phaeton in yellow with black wheels drawn by two jet-black horses. The other was an open Brake used, she knew, for servants and luggage.

She stood irresolute, wondering what she should do.

Then she heard the train move off and a Gentleman came from the platform.

He was very impressive, tall, broad-shouldered, smartly dressed with his top hat perched at an angle on his dark head.

He walked without hurrying himself to the Phaeton, and only as he reached it did Solita find her voice.

"Excuse me, Sir," she said, "but as there appears to be no conveyance here for strangers, would you be kind enough to give me a lift as far as Calver Castle?"

The Gentleman who was just about to step into his Phaeton turned to look at her.

She thought he was surprised at her appearance and she said quietly:

"I . . . I am sorry to . . . bother you, but I cannot think of any other way that I can reach the Castle."

"You are a guest there?"

"Not exactly, but I have to . . . see His Grace the Duke."

The Gentleman seemed to hesitate, until as if making up his mind he said:

"Then of course, I must take you to him."

"Thank you very much."

Solita hurried round the Phaeton to climb lithely into the other seat.

The Gentleman was already holding the reins, and almost before she had seated herself the groom who had been holding the horses' heads let them go.

He ran swiftly to climb into the seat behind.

The Phaeton was moving and she wondered what

would have happened if he had been unable to reach it.

They drove away from the Halt and now she could see the countryside was very green, the trees were coming into bud, the primroses already appearing in the hedgerows.

They drove a little way before the Gentleman said:

"You say you wish to see the Duke. I am interested to know why."

Because Solita had been appreciating the countryside, she replied without thinking:

"I wish to inform him that he is callous, selfish, insensitive, and very ungrateful!"

As she spoke she realised she had been indiscreet and added a little incoherently:

"Forgive me . . . that is . . . something I . . . should not have . . . said to a stranger."

"I am curious to know what the Duke has done to offend you."

"That is something which I shall . . . impart to His Grace," Solita answered.

They drove on some way before the Gentleman remarked:

"Surely you are very young to be travelling alone?"

He almost added:

'. . . and much too pretty!'

He had in fact been surprised when she had asked him for a lift, and he turned to see two very large blue eyes in a small heart-shaped face looking at him.

He realised her hair was the colour of sunshine.

He thought it extraordinary, looking as she did, that she should be travelling unchaperoned, even if the Calver Halt was only a short distance from London.

"I have to look after . . . myself," Solita said in answer to his question, "and that . . . too is the . . . Duke's fault!"

"I am sure he has many sins attributed to him," the Gentleman said cynically, "but I cannot conceive how he managed to overlook your need of a chaperone!"

He was laughing at her, Solita thought, and her chin went up because she considered he was impertinent.

"Do you know the Duke well?" she asked when they had driven on a little farther.

"Well enough to know he would not enjoy your condemnation of him."

"He deserves . . . everything I have said, and a good deal more!" Solita replied sharply.

"I think you are rather condemning the poor man without giving him a chance to defend himself," the Gentleman remarked.

"Some . . . things are . . . indefensible," Solita said.

She obviously did not want to say any more, and they drove quite a distance before the Gentleman asked:

"When you are not condemning Dukes for their sins, what do you do with yourself?"

"I have only just returned from abroad," Solita said, "And I think England is very beautiful."

"And you intend to stay here?"

"I think I shall have to, in which case I must find a way of keeping myself."

"Do you mean you have no money?" the Gentleman enquired.

Solita nodded before she said:

"I have been thinking what I can do, and I am sure the only possibility open to me is to be a Ballet-dancer."

The Gentleman turned his head to look at her in astonishment.

"A Ballet-dancer?" he questioned.

"I have been told that the Ballet-dancers of Covent Garden are admired and feted by the Gentleman who frequent the Clubs of St. James's."

"And that is what you want?"

Now there was no doubt of the cynicism in the way he spoke.

"It is the only real talent I have," Solita said, "except an aptitude for languages."

The Gentleman did not speak, and she went on almost as if she were speaking to herself:

"But I doubt, as I am so young, that I would be employed as a Governess, or a teacher in a School. Anyway, the English seldom bother to seek the languages of other nationalities."

"Is that what you have found in your long life?"

It was obvious the Gentleman was once again mocking her, and she replied:

"If you mean it is what I have observed—yes! When the English cannot make themselves understood by the natives whom they despise, they shout at them, but of course in English!"

The Gentleman laughed as if he could not help it.

"You are very scathing, Miss . . ."

He paused.

"Now I think of it, you have not yet told me your name."

"I see no reason why I should do so, Sir, especially as you have just pointed out, there is no Chaperone to introduce us."

The Gentleman laughed again, and it was a genuine sound of amusement.

"Very well," he said, "If you wish to be mysterious —but let me tell you—I do not think you are suited to be a Ballet-dancer!"

"Why not?" Solita asked.

"Because, unless I am mistaken, you are a Lady."

"Why should that matter if one can dance well?"

The Gentleman thought there were a number of reasons he could give her, but he chose his words carefully.

"Ballet-dancers, as you say, are feted by the Gentleman of St. James's, but they are expected to respond to the presents they receive."

Solita turned her face to look at him in surprise.

"Do you mean . . . they have to . . . thank for them?"

"They are expected to do more than thank."

"I do not . . . understand."

"Why should you?" the Gentleman enquired. "Take my advice and believe me when I tell you that a Ballet-dancer's life is not for you."

Solita sighed.

"In which case, I shall have to make the Duke do his duty, which he should have done in the first place."

"I have always believed he was very conscious of his responsibilities," the Gentleman said.

She did not reply, and after a moment he asked:

"Tell me what His Grace has done to offend you."

He spoke coaxingly in a way most women found irresistibly attractive.

Solita, however, only lifted her chin a little higher as she said:

"If I told you, I expect, because you are a friend of his, that you will try to make excuses for him!"

The Gentleman smiled.

"I think he is quite capable of making his own."

"And I am sure he will be very plausible!" Solita said, and now she was the one who was sarcastic.

"What has happened," the Gentleman enquired, "that

the Duke refuses to help you, as you seem to consider he should do?"

There was silence, and after a moment he said:

"Perhaps you are thinking you might appeal to me!"

Once again Solita turned to look at him, and he was aware from the astonishment in her eyes that she had never thought of such a thing.

"No . . . of course . . . not!" she exclaimed. "I would not think of . . . imposing myself on a . . . stranger!"

She paused before she went on:

"I suppose really it was incorrect of me to ask you if you would give me a lift, but I had not thought there would not be a Hackney Carriage at the Halt, and I knew of no other way to reach the Castle."

She sounded so worried at what she seemed to think was an indiscretion that the Gentleman said soothingly:

"It was actually the sensible thing to do, and it would have been very foolish of you to let me drive away."

"In which case, I might have had to walk," Solita said logically. "How far is it to the Castle?"

"Over three miles."

"Oh, dear, and I should not have known the way."

"So you see, you did the only sensible thing," the Gentleman remarked, "and I must thank you for making my drive more interesting than it would otherwise have been."

Solita gave a little laugh.

"Now you are definitely being kind to me and making me feel less guilty."

"That does not make me less curious," the Gentleman said. "And may I add that if you are in trouble, I should like to help you."

"That is something the Duke . . . has to . . . do!" Solita said firmly.

There was a determination in the way she spoke that amused the Gentleman. It as unusual in one so young.

"You say you have been living abroad," he said, "but I know you are English. Are you glad to be back in your mother country?"

"In a way," Solita said. "Even though it is strange, and rather frightening, especially—"

She stopped as if she thought that once again she was being indiscreet.

"You have no money," the Gentleman finished.

"I have a little," Solita said, "but it will not last for ever."

"That is what we have all found at one time or another."

"So you understand that is why I have to think about myself," Solita said.

She looked at him pleadingly as she said:

"I really do dance very well. The Dancing Master at my School said once that I was as good as any professional and that is what made me think of trying to get employment in a Ballet in Covent Garden."

She looked at him a little anxiously as she said:

"That is . . . the best in London . . . is it . . . not?"

"I have always heard so," the Gentleman said, "but I have already told you—forget the idea."

"Because I am a Lady? I cannot believe they would turn me away just because of that!"

"They would not turn you away if you really dance as well as you think you do," the Gentleman said, "but it is not the life for somebody who is gentle and well-born, and educated, as you obviously are."

Solita sighed.

"Then how do Ladies, if they . . . need money . . . earn it?"

"Ladies get married when they are your age, and there must be somebody who could introduce you to the Social World?"

"I do not want to enter the Social World," Solita said, "what I really want is enough money so that I can go to India."

"To India?" the Gentleman exclaimed. "Why on earth should you want to go to India?"

"For a very special reason of my own."

The Gentleman was just about to ask her what it was when she gave a little cry.

"Surely that is the Castle!" she exclaimed. "It is exactly how I thought it would look!"

Some way ahead of them, standing on an incline so that it was above the flat meadowland through which they were passing, was Calver Castle.

With trees protectingly around it, and the sunshine shining on the old tower, it looked like a jewel in a velvet setting.

The ancient Castle that had been built in Norman times was still there.

Generation after generation had however added their own ideas to the original building, until in the eighteenth century the hotch-potch had been swept away.

A magnificent piece of Paladian architecture had taken its place.

Now there was a centre block with wings stretching out on either side of it.

Only the grey tower stone was different from the white stone of the new mansion.

The sun was glinting on what seemed to Solita to be a hundred windows, and from this distance it looked as if the whole Castle had stepped out of a Fairy Story.

"It is . . . beautiful!" she said in a low voice.

"I thought you would admire it," the Gentleman remarked.

"How could anybody live in such a magnificent place and not have a character to match it?" Solita asked.

Now it was obvious that she was thinking scathingly of the Duke.

The Gentleman's eyes were twinkling as they drove on.

They turned in through enormous wrought-iron gates with lodges on either side of them.

They drove down a long avenue of oak trees.

At the end they crossed a bridge over the lake and up an incline which led to the Castle itself.

"I must thank you, Sir, for bringing me here," Solita said, "and I am extremely grateful that I did not have to walk!"

"You would certainly not have got here so quickly," the Gentleman replied dryly.

"Thank you very, very much."

He was still holding the reins. Solita did not attempt to shake hands with him.

She climbed out of the Phaeton, assisted by one of the flunkeys who at their approach had come down the long flight of steps from the front door.

The steps, Solita saw, were covered with a red carpet.

Only when she had walked a little way up them did she realise that the Gentleman who had driven her here was following her.

He reached her side and they walked through the front door together.

"Nice to see you back, Your Grace," an elderly Butler said.

As he spoke Solita turned to look at the Gentleman with accusing eyes.

She was about to say something when the Duke said:

"The Lady I have with me, Dawson, would, I am sure, like to wash and tidy herself after the journey, and we will have tea in the Blue Salon."

"Very good, Your Grace."

The Butler went to Solita's side, saying respectfully:

"Will you come this way, Madam?"

He proceeded her up the stairs, and as she followed him she was too amazed to think clearly.

"How could I have guessed," she asked herself, "that the Duke would be on the train like an ordinary passenger?"

She had always understood that Dukes in England had their own private trains, or, alternatively, a coach to themselves which was attached to the Express.

She had not thought that everyone who stopped at the Halt would be going to the Castle or that any man might easily be the Duke himself.

An elderly Housekeeper escorted her to a very impressive bedroom.

After she had washed her hands and tidied her hair she was escorted to the top of the stairs and saw the Butler waiting for her in the hall below.

She had taken off her hat at the suggestion of the housekeeper.

But, because she thought after what she had said the Duke might easily send her away immediately, she carried it in her hand.

"How could I have been so foolish as to have talked so indiscreetly?" she asked herself.

At the same time, she remembered that it was what she had intended to say to the Duke anyway.

If he had heard it already, then it did not matter one way or the other.

She wondered frantically however that, if he was angry, where she could stay the night.

She had the uncomfortable feeling that as she was unchaperoned it might be difficult to get into any respectable hotel.

Yet, she told herself as she went down the stairs, she was not going to be intimidated by the Duke!

It was all his fault that she was here.

The old Butler smiled at her as he said:

"His Grace is waiting for you in the Blue Salon, Madam, and I'm sure you could do with a cup of tea after your journey?"

"I would enjoy it very much," Solita said.

She thought the old man would be surprised if she told him it would be the first tea she had drunk since she had come to England.

They walked a little way along a high and very impressive corridor.

Then Dawson opened a door, and without announcing Solita, as he did not know her name, she walked in.

The Duke was standing in front of the fireplace, and Solita thought as she walked towards him that he looked rather intimidating.

There was however an undoubted look of defiance in her blue eyes as she stopped opposite him and curtsied.

"I suppose I should apologise," she said, "but you have altered so much since I last saw you that it was . . . impossible for me to . . . recognise you."

"Since you last saw me?" the Duke enquired. "And when was that?"

Almost despite herself, Solita smiled.

"It was ten years ago, and while I was much smaller,

you were always laughing and I thought I could . . . trust you."

The Duke stared at her.

"Ten years ago?" he repeated.

Suddenly his expression changed.

"You are not telling me," he said almost incredulously, "that you are Charles Gresham's daughter?"

"I am. I am Solita Gresham, who you have forgotten about!"

"That is not quite true," the Duke replied, "but why are you here and what has happened to my Cousin Mildred."

"Your Cousin Mildred, whom Your Grace has ignored completely ever since I went to live with her, died a month ago."

"I had no idea. I was not informed."

"There was no one to inform you but me, and it was when I found that I had no money that I came to England to ask you what you had done with what Papa left me."

The Duke put his hand up to his forehead.

"This is all completely bewildering," he said. "After I left you with my Cousin I thought I arranged for your father's money to be sent to her regularly in order to pay for your schooling."

"As far as I am aware, she never had a penny!" Solita retorted. "And she paid for everything herself."

"It is hard to believe that what you are telling me is the truth."

"I can assure Your Grace I should not have troubled you if I had not found on your Cousin's death that her money came from a Trust Fund. It ceased as soon as she was not there to receive it."

"Are you telling me you are left penniless?"

"I sold some jewellery, which your Cousin had given me over the years, to pay for my fare to England."

"There has obviously been some hideous mistake," the Duke said, "and my only excuse is that after I left you in Naples I was sent with a batallion of my Regiment to the West Indies."

He thought as he spoke of the last time he had seen Solita, when she had flung her arms around his neck and kissed him goodbye.

An enchanting child aged eight, he had looked after her on the voyage home from India.

Looking back now, he could understand why she had spoken so scathingly about him.

Charles Gresham had been a Captain in the Army when he was a young Subaltren.

Gresham had befriended him from the moment he had arrived in India, and they had a great many tastes in common.

They had been moved up to the North West Frontier. Gresham's wife and daughter had not been allowed to accompany him.

They had had a gruelling time with the tribesmen.

They were hard fighting men who were continually incited to rebel against the English by the Russians who had infiltrated into Afghanistan.

During one night-attack which had come unexpectedly, the enemy had outnumbered the British.

Charles Gresham had saved the Duke's life. In doing so he had received a wound to his thigh.

They had left for Peshawar together.

It was while Charles Gresham was convalescent that he became involved with a very beautiful woman who appeared to be infatuated with him.

The Duke, who was at that time only Hugo Leigh,

never suspected she had another reason for pursuing Gresham, as he was a very attractive man.

When Gresham had recovered from his wounds he went back to his Unit.

The Duke was ordered to stay on in Peshawar for another week.

Afterwards, despite an official enquiry, it was difficult to ascertain exactly what had happened.

All that was known was that a company of British soldiers had been ambushed with Gresham among them. All of them had lost their lives.

It was only when the attractive woman who had seemed infatuated with Gresham disappeared that it was whispered that she was a Russian spy.

It was then that the Duke had become suspicious.

There was nothing he could prove, and when he went to Lucknow, Mrs. Gresham was waiting for him.

He learnt that she had heard the rumours that were being circulated amongst the British troops.

Because she was broken-hearted at losing her husband, there was little the Duke could say to comfort her.

He had to admit that the woman who had been in her husband's company was under suspicion.

Although Mrs. Gresham was very brave about it, he knew that she was certain, as he was, the Russian was a spy and she had wormed out of Charles Gresham the orders he had been given, which had sent him to his death.

It was when the Duke was in Lucknow that he received a telegram from England informing him that his mother was ill.

Having obtained compassionate leave, he left on the first available ship from Bombay and found that Mrs.

Gresham and her small daughter were also on their way to England.

He had been a close friend of Charles Gresham, who also saved his life.

The Duke was therefore eager to do everything in his power to make the voyage as comfortable as possible for his widow.

He was aware that Mrs. Gresham would face a lonely future without her husband.

They talked over what she should do and where she could live, and he learnt she was not only poor, but had very few relatives.

They discussed it as they passed through the Red Sea, and when they went ashore at Port Sudan.

Then the ship moved slowly up the newly-opened Suez Canal.

By the time they reached Alexandria the Duke was aware that Mrs. Gresham had caught a pernicious fever, perhaps at the native Bazaar they had visited.

The Ship's Doctor could do little for her.

He only insisted that Solita be moved into another cabin and kept away from her mother until the infection was over.

She therefore spent her time with Hugo Leigh and several other Officers who were on board.

They spoilt her, bought her chocolates, and played games with her.

She was an exceedingly attractive child, looking like a small angel with her golden hair and bright blue eyes.

She ran swiftly about the deck with a grace that made her seem as if she were flying.

One evening the Duke remembered she had danced gracefully in the Saloon to the music that one of the Officers was playing on the piano.

When Solita began to dance it was an unconscious expression of the joy the music brought to her.

She did not seem to be aware that she had an audience.

In fact, it was only when she stopped dancing and everybody applauded that she realised that they had been watching her.

He had thought she was unusually talented for a young child, and he could understand now why she thought she could be a Ballet-dancer.

Mrs. Gresham had died three days after they had left Alexandria.

Solita had cried on Hugo Leigh's shoulder, but there was little he could do to comfort her.

"What . . . will happen . . . to me . . . now?" she asked piteously.

Then with a little cry of horror she said:

"I will . . . not be . . . sent to an . . . Orphanage?"

Hugo Leigh had known she was afraid, having seen the Orphanages in India.

The children, whilst adequately fed, were very strictly disciplined.

For a moment his arms had tightened around the frail little body as he said:

"I promise you that will not happen."

"Then . . . where shall . . . I go?"

The Duke could see her face now, the tears running down her cheeks.

And yet, in some way it made her even prettier than she had been when she was smiling.

"I will think of something," he said.

"You . . . promise? You . . . promise?" she asked.

"I promise," he answered, and wondered how he could keep it.

It was only when they reached Naples that he remembered that a Cousin of his father's—Mildred Leigh, lived in Sorrento.

She was nearly sixty and, because she suffered from rheumatism, the Doctors had advised her to live in a warm climate.

She was a kind woman who had never married, and was therefore often lonely, especially as she lived in a foreign country.

On an impulse the Duke took Solita to see her.

His Cousin had immediately understood the problem and offered to have Solita with her.

"It would give me a great deal of happiness, dear boy," she told the Duke. "I will send her to one of the best Schools in Naples, and I have a feeling she will grow up to be a beauty."

It had all seemed very satisfactory, and it was only when he was leaving that Solita clung to him feverishly.

He had known it was because he was the one thing she had left of the life that belonged to her father and mother.

"You . . . will not . . . forget me?" she pleaded. "You will . . . come and see me . . . again . . . soon?"

"As soon as I can," he promised, "but you must remember I am a soldier, like your father."

"But . . . you will . . . think of . . . me?"

"II promise I will do that."

He had kissed her goodbye.

He could remember now seeing a pathetic little figure with tears in her eyes standing on the steps of his Cousin's Villa.

He had written to Solita over several months and he had sent her postcards.

Then he had been posted to the West Indies.

After two years there he was sent back to India on a special mission.

It was in Calcutta he learnt incredibly something he had never expected had occurred.

He had become the fourth Duke of Calverleigh.

His father had been the younger son of the third Duke, and as was traditional kept on very short commons, while his elder brother had everything.

It had not worried Hugo Leigh, who was perfectly content with his life as a soldier.

What happened had therefore come as a complete bombshell.

His grandfather the Duke and his Uncle, the Marquis of Calver, had both been drowned when crossing the Irish Sea in a storm.

They had been on their way to Ireland to stay with the Viceroy.

They wished to buy horses to improve the Duke's racing stables.

Hugo Leigh had hurried home from India and found there was a great deal for him to do, not only in the Castle, but in his position in the country and in Court circles.

Queen Victoria had welcomed him at Windsor, and the change in his life was fantastic.

From being an unimportant Captain he found himself a wealthy man and the owner of one of the finest houses in England.

The Duke admitted that he had forgotten Solita.

He had written when he first reached England to his Solicitors telling them to investigate what was left of Charles Gresham's estate.

They were to make sure the money was properly invested for the child of the marriage.

After that, he now confessed, he had done nothing, imagining that if anything was wrong, his Cousin Mildred would notify him.

As he looked at Solita's accusing eyes, he told himself he had been very remiss and he could only say:

"I am sorry, Solita, and I hope you will forgive me."

"You promised you would not forget me," she said.

He thought for a moment it was the child of eight who had kissed him goodbye speaking.

"I know," he said, "and I am very contrite, but I did have a lot to think about."

"I expected at least that you would write to me every Christmas," Solita said, "and Aunt Mildred was hurt because you never sent her a card after the first year I was with her."

The Duke sat down beside her on the sofa.

"Supposing you pour me a cup of tea," he said, "then we will talk about the future. However many regrets we have, we cannot undo the past."

"That is true," Solita agreed, "but I have been . . . hating you for so long that it is going to be difficult to feel . . . anything else."

The Duke laughed.

"That sounds very intimidating!" he said. "At the same time, you are now in England, and starting a new life altogether."

Solita poured out his tea and a cup for herself, then she said:

"Surely Papa left . . . some money, otherwise I will have to be a . . . Ballet-dancer."

"You will be nothing of the sort!" the Duke said. "I am your Guardian, and it is something I will definitely not allow!"

"Did you say you are my Guardian?" Solita asked.

"Of course I am," he replied, "Your mother put you in my charge and I took you to my Cousin. If I have neglected my responsibilities during the last years, I must make up for them now."

Solita frowned.

"I did not . . . mean to be an . . . encumbrance," she said. "I just thought . . . you could give me the . . . money that was Papa's . . . and I would . . . find myself . . . something to do."

"What you are going to do," the Duke said firmly, "is to shine in the Social World in which you are not interested!"

"I want to go to India."

"That may be possible later," the Duke replied, "but why, particularly?"

He thought she was not going to reply, then she said:

"I want to . . . avenge Papa!"

"You want to do—what?" the Duke enquired.

"Avenge Papa! It was the Russians who killed him, and one day I intend to avenge his death!"

The Duke stared at her.

"How on earth do you think you can do that?" he enquired.

Solita looked at him in a strange way, as if she were looking, he thought, into his heart.

"You loved Papa," she said in a low voice, "and you know that Russian woman behaved . . . treacherously and caused his . . . death and that of his men."

Her lips tightened for a moment before she went on in a hard voice:

"Only when I have killed her . . . or a Russian like her . . . will I feel that Papa did . . . not die in . . . vain!"

chapter two

THE Duke stared at her in astonishment. Then he asked:

"Are you serious?"

"I am very serious," Solita replied, "and I think you, of all people, should have tried to avenge Papa's death, especially when he saved your life."

"Killing a man in battle is one thing, but killing at other times is murder!" the Duke said firmly.

"I know that," Solita replied, "but ever since I heard from Mama exactly what happened, and also, as it happens, from you, I was determined that Papa's death should not go unavenged."

The Duke sat back in his chair and crossed his legs.

"Now let us reason this out," he said. "You must realise such an idea coming from a young girl such as yourself is not only foolish but extremely dangerous!"

Solita looked at him with what he thought was a contemptuous expression on her face.

But she did not speak, and after a little while he went on:

"I am sorry that I neglected you for so long, and I shall certainly find out exactly what money your father has left you, but I think, if you are honest, you will agree that you have been well cared for by my Cousin."

"Aunt Mildred, as she asked me to call her, was

wonderful!" Solita admitted. "She sent me to the best School in Naples, and I made a great many friends there who were extremely useful."

"Useful?" the Duke questioned.

Solita smiled.

"The girls were of different nationalities and from all over Euorpe, and they each helped me to learn their language."

"You said you had an aptitude for languages," the Duke said, "but I am afraid you will not find it a great advantage socially."

Again he thought Solita looked at him contemptuously.

It was something which was very unusual where women were concerned.

The Duke did not have to be conceited to realise that he not only attracted women because of his title, but also because he was a very handsome man.

It suddenly struck him that Solita had not recognised him and because he was curious he said:

"As you remember so much about your mother and father who died when you were very young, I am rather surprised that you did not remember me."

"You have changed!"

"Changed?" the Duke questioned. "Of course—I have grown older."

"It is not only that."

"Then what is it?"

He spoke a little aggressively, feeling it extraordinary that this young girl should see a great difference in him.

Granted it was ten years since they had met, it was not surprising if he did not recognise her.

But he imagined that now, at thirty-one, he was very much the same as he had been as a Subaltern who had received his baptism of fire on the North West Frontier.

He realised that Solita was contemplating him in a serious manner which meant she was thinking out how she could explain to him the difference.

After a while she said:

"I think the main difference in you is that when you looked after me in the ship, especially after Mama's death, I could feel how friendly and understanding you were."

"And now?" the Duke asked as if he could not help himself.

"You are reserved, cynical, and, I suspect, bored!"

The Duke stared at her.

"I want to deny I am any of those things!"

"You asked me a question, and I thought you wanted a truthful answer," Solita said.

"I think you are prejudiced because you are angry with me for neglecting you."

"I realise now it was a question of 'forgetting' me!" Solita retorted. "And, of course, Aunt Mildred, who had been so kind."

The Duke thought he was tired of apologising.

Although he admitted he was in the wrong, he resented being taken to task by someone so young, and, in fact, so pretty.

He rose from his chair and walked across the room to pull the bell.

There was silence until the door opened and Dawson stood there.

"Miss Solita Gresham will be staying here as my guest," the Duke said. "Have her trunks taken upstairs and unpacked."

"Very good, Your Grace."

The door shut and the Duke looked at Solita.

To his surprise, her eyes were twinkling.

"I am very grateful to be offered a bed for the night," she said. "I was rather afraid I might have to stay at an Hotel, which I cannot really afford."

"Where did you stay last night?" the Duke enquired.

"In the train that arrived at Calais very late. The passengers stayed in their compartments, and boarded the ship at dawn."

"What happened after that?"

"I took the train to London and went straight to Calverleigh House."

"You knew I had become the Duke?"

"Aunt Mildred had the English newspapers sent out every week," Solita explained.

"What did they tell you at my house?" he asked.

"They said you had left for the country and were at the Castle, so I drove straight to the station, caught the train with only two minutes to spare, and had no idea that you were on it!"

The Duke did not speak, and she added after a moment:

"I always thought Dukes, like Royalty, travelled in their own trains."

"I came to the country at a moment's notice," the Duke explained, "and therefore had to be content with just a reserved carriage."

Solita laughed.

"That must have been a 'come-down!'"

"I was not so grand when you first knew me."

"That is true," Solita agreed. "I remember you telling me how cramped your cabin was in the ship and that you had to share it with two other officers."

She looked round the room and said almost as if she spoke to herself:

"Now you own this magnificent Castle!"

"Which will be your home for the moment," the Duke said.

Solita looked at him in surprise.

"You are asking me to stay here?"

"I have been thinking," the Duke said, "that as both your parents are dead, and I promised your mother I would look after you. I am, after all, your Guardian."

He saw the suspicion of a smile on Solita's lips and said hastily:

"All right, rather a remiss one, but I intend to take up my duties better late than never!"

"But if I do not want you as my Guardian?" Solita asked.

"I am afraid there is very little you can do about it," the Duke replied. "The rules of Guardianship are very strict in England, and I think I can prove in any Court of Law that that is my official position where you are concerned."

"And what is mine?" Solita questioned.

"That is quite simple," the Duke replied. "You have to obey me!"

She gave a little laugh.

"Now I see where all this is leading, and what you intend to do is to forbid me to go to India so that I can avenge my father."

"I am certainly going to discourage you from doing anything so stupid as the latter," the Duke said. "I intend that you shall take your rightful place in the Social World as my Ward, which is a very different thing."

There was a pause for a moment. Then he said:

"I am going to ask my maternal grandmother, the Countess of Milborne, to chaperon you at the weekend, but I have guests arriving today who will chaperon you

26

until we return to London, and you can meet her."

He thought as he spoke that he had coped satisfactorily with the problem of Solita.

The next step was to get in touch with his Solicitors to find out what had been done about Charles Gresham's estate.

He could not help thinking after Mrs. Gresham had said they were very poor that there was unlikely to be much money for Solita.

That information could wait, however, until he returned to London.

He walked to his desk to find, as he expected, a list of the guests he had invited had been put there by his Secretary.

It was only when he picked it up that he remembered the reason for the party.

It had actually been planned for two important guests who were in fact Russian.

He told himself this was certainly unfortunate in view of what Solita had just said.

Then he told himself the foolish child could not be serious.

She certainly could not extend her desire for revenge on every Russian she met.

He read the list through, starting with the names of his English friends. He told Solita who they were.

"They are older than you," he said, "but, of course, another time I will include a number of young people in my party. But you will meet three of the most beautiful women in London, which is something, I am sure, you will enjoy."

"I am sure I shall," Solita said. "Aunt Mildred used to read me the Court Columns, and I think I have seen pictures in English magazines of two of the Ladies you have just mentioned."

"There are two other guests," the Duke added casually, "the Princess Zenka Kozlovski, and her brother Prince Ivan Vlasov."

There was a silence.

After a moment Solita asked:

"Are you saying . . . they are Russians?"

"Yes, they are Russians," the Duke confirmed, "and I hope, Solita, you will have the good manners to behave with propriety towards two important people who are my guests."

His voice was serious as he went on:

"The Princess is a very beautiful and charming person, and although I have not met her brother, Prince Ivan, I have heard him spoken of in most flattering terms."

He paused so there could be no mistake as he added:

"You will therefore understand that I would not wish to think they had been insulted in my house."

"How can you entertain . . . Russians," Solita asked, "when you know they are . . . responsible for . . . killing so many of our . . . soldiers on the North West Frontier!"

"Officially," the Duke reminded her, "it is the tribesmen who are causing the trouble."

"But you know as well as I do," Solita retorted, "that it is the Russians in Afghanistan who are inciting the tribesmen."

"I am well aware of that," the Duke said coldly, "but we are not at war with Russia."

"But surely, anyone of any intelligence knows that they want eventually to invade India!"

The Duke looked at her in astonishment.

"How can you know that?"

"I have listened to the Italians, the French, and the Spanish talking about it. Their Statesmen think that the British are living in a 'Fool's Paradise' in thinking it is ours, and that no one can take it from us!"

"I think it is unlikely," the Duke said.

"Russia is a very large country," Solita said. "They are ambitious, and also very . . . resentful of . . . British power."

The Duke looked at her with raised eyebrows.

"How can you talk like this?" he asked. "Who has been telling you about these things?"

Solita gave a little laugh and spread out her arms.

"It is only the British like yourself who think that the Europeans are blind, deaf, and dumb!"

"I think nothing of the sort!" the Duke said sharply. "At the same time, it is a mistake for you to have your head stuffed with a lot of rubbish."

"What you are really saying is that I should be listening to the exaggerated compliments of young men," Solita said, "and thinking about clothes rather than politics."

The Duke laughed. Then he asked:

"Do politics interest you so much?"

"Yes," she replied, "and certainly where they concern Russia!"

"I think this obsession with Russia is a mistake," the Duke said crossly.

"Then we will not talk about it," Solita said, "and I promise I will be polite to your Russians, even while I want to thrust a knife into them or shoot them!"

"You are not to talk like that!" the Duke admonished. "I do not believe for one moment that you mean it, and I think you are just showing off."

He thought surprisingly that she did not seem in the least abashed at the way he spoke.

He therefore added in an even more serious tone:

"Please behave like a Lady, and let me hear no more of your animosity towards the Russians as a race."

"Very well, Your Grace."

Solita spoke with a humility that he was sure she assumed, and to make certain she understood he said:

"As your Guardian, and as I think the only person you have to turn to at this moment, it would be a far more comfortable situation if we are friends."

Solita smiled at him.

"I am trying to be friendly, but I am missing the happy, charming young officer who used to play games with me on the deck and who carried me to bed when I was too tired to go on dancing."

There was something wistful in the way she spoke.

The Duke suddenly had the idea that perhaps all those years ago she had idolised him.

After all, he was the one person after her parents had died who knew anything about her, and to whom she could turn for love and understanding.

He sat down beside her and held out his hand.

"Let us go back to those days when you trusted me, and I promise I will look after and help you, as I did then."

It would have been very difficult for any woman to resist the Duke when he was appealing to her.

Still a little reluctant, Solita put her hand into his.

She felt the firmness and strength of his fingers, then he said:

"I think your father would be glad that you are here with me, and I am sure your mother would be."

She looked up at him.

He knew that she was wondering whether she could trust him, or whether he would let her down as he had done before.

Then as if he willed her to do so, she said:

"I will try . . . to behave as you . . . want, although it may be . . . difficult where the . . . Russians are . . . concerned."

"I am sure when you met them you will realise they have nothing in common with the Russians who you think are threatening India."

He felt her fingers quiver in his and he added:

"In the meantime, Solita, enjoy yourself. You have new worlds to conquer, and as you are very lovely, I do not think you will find it a difficult task."

"Do not be too optimistic," Solita said. "I am well aware of my shortcomings."

"I have not noticed any as yet," the Duke remarked.

He released her hand and rose to his feet.

"You have had a very long journey," he said, "and what I am going to suggest now is that you rest before dinner which will not be until eight o'clock."

He paused for a moment to explain:

"My friends will not be arriving at the Halt until after six, and they will be travelling in my private carriage, which because I did not wish to come with them was why I came ahead."

Solita got to her feet.

"I suppose," she said, "it was not only because you were travelling as an ordinary passenger that I did not think you were the Duke, I was also expecting you to be wearing your coronet!"

The Duke laughed.

"I am humiliated that you think me so unimportant without all the trappings."

"I would not have been deceived had I seen you against the background of this beautiful Palace," Solita replied, "or perhaps I was expecting you to look as you did ten years ago, in badly fitting shorts, playing deck-tennis with me."

The Duke laughed, and as she reached the door Solita looked back to say:

"I thought then that you were the most attractive man I had ever met!"

The Duke tried to think of a suitable retort, but she had gone.

He was aware that she had said "then," making it quite certain that he did not qualify for the description now.

"She is certainly very unusual," he told himself.

He had never expected a young girl to talk in such a way, and he must certainly not allow her to carry out her intention of committing murder.

He tried to reassure himself that his explanation was the correct one and that Solita was just "showing off."

Even if the opportunity presented itself, it was unlikely that she would know how to kill a person.

He suspected it was just part of her plan to make him feel guilty because he had neglected her.

After all, it was true that her father had saved his life.

It was therefore extremely remiss of him to have forgotten her for so long.

He had, as he had told her, been hurried off to the West Indies.

When he had returned, he had been engaged on the development of a weapon for the Army which was a Top Secret.

He found himself working nearly twenty-four hours a

day, and only when he unexpectedly came into the title had he resigned from the Army.

He then had a great many personal things to occupy his mind. Although he had no intention of telling Solita about it, he was involved at the moment in a secret investigation.

Three days ago the Earl of Kimberley, who was Secretary of State for Foreign Affairs, had sent for him.

The Earl welcomed the Duke when he called on him at the Foreign Office.

A handsome and very distinguished-looking man age fifty-seven, he had known the Duke since he was a young boy at Eton with his son John.

The Duke had actually been John Wodehouse's fag at Eton.

He had stayed with him at the family house in Norfolk, where the Kimberleys had always made him welcome.

In the following years the Earl of Kimberley became more and more important.

He was Under-Secretary of State for Foreign Affairs, Envoy to Russian and to Copenhagen, Under-Secretary of State for India, Lord Lieutenant of Ireland, and Lord Privy Seal.

Now, as Secretary of State for India, he was, the Duke thought, exactly the right person for a very difficult and intricate job.

"I am delighted to see you, Hugo!" he said. "And thank you for coming so quickly."

"Your letter sounded rather like the cry of a drowning man shouting for a lifeline!" the Duke replied.

"Come and sit down," the Earl invited.

He moved from his desk towards some comfortable armchairs arranged either side of the fireplace.

There was a seriousness in his expression which made the Duke feel uneasily that he was going to be asked to do something not only inconvenient, but also extremely dangerous.

He had often, in the last few years, obliged the India Office by undertaking secret investigations on their behalf.

One had involved him in discovering a new weapon suspected of being made in Afghanistan with Russian money.

It meant him being away from England for about three months, travelling in the most uncomfortable conditions imaginable.

Finally he had nearly lost his life when he had blown up a gun together with those who had been designing it.

His last mission had taken place only six months earlier.

Again, after a great deal of physical discomfort, he had succeeded in identifying a man who had been hiding from the British in Finland, and had brought him to justice.

"Whatever Kimberley suggests," the Duke told himself, "the answer is 'No'!"

Then, as the Secretary of State seemed to have some difficulty in finding words, the Duke said:

"If you are going to suggest that I climb the Himalayas or wear a disguise which involves walking barefoot through Arabia, the answer is 'No'!"

The Earl laughed.

"It is not quite as bad as that this time, but I desperately need your help."

"Why?" the Duke asked shortly.

"Because I know of no one as clever as you are when

it comes to identifying people and solving a conundrum which has defeated all of us."

"I would like to help you," the Duke said, "but I really am busy with my own affairs."

"I am aware of that," the Earl said disarmingly, "and that is why I have hesitated to ask you until I was sure no one else could discover what I have to find out."

"You are trying to make me curious," the Duke said accusingly, "and I tell you frankly, I am growing too old to sleep on rocky ground or in some filthy cave which has been used by animals! I prefer my own bed!"

"Or that of someone very attractive," the Earl said.

The Duke laughed.

"Who has been telling tales?"

"I have heard a whisper that you are somewhat engaged with a very beautiful Princess!"

The Duke smiled as he said:

"Exactly, My Lord! And I have no intention of leaving the field clear for my rivals!"

"I would not ask you to do so," the Earl said, "what I am asking you is if you will find out for me if there is a leak in this Office."

The Duke stared at him in astonishment.

"A leak in this office?" he exclaimed.

"Somebody, and I cannot find out who it is," the Earl of Kimberley said, "is costing us the lives of a large number of our men in India."

He spoke very seriously and the Duke asked:

"If that is true, surely you must have some idea of who has access to secret information?"

"If it were as easy as that, I would have discovered the culprit by now," the Earl replied, "but I have had every person in the Office investigated, also in the building, and as we have come up with nothing, I am asking you, Hugo, to find out what is happening."

Despite himself, the Duke was intrigued.

"Tell me from the beginning."

"It started about six months ago," the Earl began, "when the Viceroy informed us that a plan to reinforce the troops on the North West Frontier which had been sent from us to him and on to the Officer-in-Charge must have been intercepted."

"How?" the Duke questioned.

"The troops were moved with every possible precaution," the Earl explained. "The men themselves thought they were going to quite a different destination from what was intended, and the Officer-in-Charge received his correct orders only after they had actually started out for the Fort they were to reinforce."

"What happened?" the Duke asked.

"They were ambushed and practically every man lost his life! It took place so quickly and was so well planned that it was quite obviously masterminded by someone far more experienced than tribesmen!"

"You mean—it was the Russians who planned it!" the Duke remarked.

"Exactly!" the Earl said.

He paused for a moment to say:

"The same thing happened in January and again last month. The last time it would have been utterly impossible for the enemy to be in any strength in the place where the battle took place unless they had previous information that our troops were being moved."

He made a very eloquent gesture with his hand before he said:

"I need not bother you with every detail. Suffice it to say that it is impossible to ignore the fact that information is being relayed to the enemy before it reaches India."

"What do you want me to do about it?"

"That is what I am asking you," the Earl replied. "I swear to you, Hugo, I have tried everything possible to discover the truth. I have had to take into my confidence one or two of my older colleagues whom I can trust implicitly."

He paused for a moment, then added:

"I have, of course, also told my son John, who I am hoping will later follow in my footsteps. But it has all been to no avail, and we have failed."

He looked at the Duke for some seconds before he went on:

"I am afraid, actually afraid to send messages in code because every time I do so it means the loss of more British lives."

There was an expression in his voice as he spoke which showed how much it hurt him, and he went on:

"I have coded the messages myself so that they would pass through as few hands as possible, but last month I learned that that, too, had been a failure."

"If I had not known you for so long, and I did not know how extremely efficient and punctilious you are, I would find your story impossible to believe!"

"It is true—dammit—it is true!" the Earl said. "And how can I go on allowing our men to die simply because we have a spy in our midst?"

"I understand your feelings," the Duke said.

"And you will help me?"

The Duke twisted his lips before he said dryly:

"I suppose I shall have to—but God knows how!"

"You have been so successful in the past," the Earl said. "You have often succeeded where everybody else has failed, and I can only beg you on my knees not to fail us now!"

"I have a feeling you are asking too much," the Duke said, "and as you know, on the other occasions when I have helped you, it has been more by luck than anything else."

"You are very modest all of a sudden!" The Earl smiled, then added, "but you know as well as I do that you have an instinct which few other people have."

He paused before he said:

"Some men have it where pictures are concerned. They will ferret out an Old Master that has been hidden under the dirt and grime of centuries."

The Duke smiled because he knew it was true, and the Earl went on:

"Explorers tell me they have the same instinct when they find a statue that has been buried for over a thousand years, or a vase that has been thrown onto the dungheap by someone with no idea that it originated in Ancient Greece!"

"I am not an expert in any of those things," the Duke admitted.

"Perhaps not," the Earl replied, "but you have an uncanny aptitude for recognising a man who has changed his whole identity and even the colour of his skin."

"I have also had my failures," the Duke remarked dryly.

"If you have, I have not heard of them," the Earl replied, "and what I am asking you to do now is to find the man who is receiving secrets from this building— secrets which in the wrong hands are more deadly than a bullet!"

The Duke sighed.

"I suppose, as you are so persuasive, that I shall have to agree to do what you want, and although you have put your trust in me, I am afraid you are going to be disappointed."

The Earl's face lit up.

"You mean you will help me?"

"You make it impossible for me to refuse!"

"Thank you," the Earl said with a sigh of relief. "I do not mind telling you, Hugo, it is a problem that has kept me wake night after night. Now, for the first time for a long time, I shall be able to sleep peacefully."

"For God's sake, do not do that!" the Duke retorted. "I cannot work in the dark alone. I want a list of every person who is employed in this building together with your personal comments on them."

"You shall have it within twenty-four hours," the Earl promised.

"I need, too, to know exactly the procedure by which all secret information is relayed outside. I know how it operates from this end."

"Yes, of course," the Earl agreed quickly.

The Duke rose to his feet.

"As far as anybody else is aware, I have come here today to ask you to stay with me and to give out the prizes in the local Horse Show two weeks from now."

"Good Lord!" the Earl ejaculated. "Do I have to do that?"

"Can you think of a better reason why I should have come here in person?" the Duke asked.

The Earl nodded his head to show he understood, and said as they walked to the door:

"I cannot thank you enough. I know it is an imposition to ask for your help once again, but I am really desperate!"

"Then we must just keep our fingers crossed," the Duke replied lightly, "and remember when I have gone to say what a bore I am to make you give away the prizes!"

"I shall certainly say that with an element of truth in my voice!" the Earl replied.

The Duke laughed.

As he opened the door he said in a voice loud enough to be heard by the people in the corridor and those in the office opposite whose door was open:

"I am very grateful to you, My Lord, for saying you will officiate at my Local Horse Show. I can now have the leaflets printed, and I am sure we shall have a record number of entrants, thanks to you!"

"I must say," the Earl replied, "you put a heavy strain on our friendship, and I am a very busy man."

"Nonsense!" the Duke said, laughing. "It will do you good to get out into the fresh air for a change! You are beginning to look older than your years, being incarcerated in this musty old place!"

"You insult me!" the Earl replied.

They were both laughing as they walked towards the door where the Duke's Phaeton was waiting for him.

"Look at those horses," he said, "do they not make you envious?"

"I shall look forward to riding one of your best Arab-bred stallions," the Earl replied, "so do not disappoint me."

"I will not do that," the Duke promised.

He walked down the steps of the India Office and climbed into his Phaeton.

When he looked back, the Earl waved to him.

Then as the Secretary of State walked back to his office, those whom he passed could hear him muttering:

"Damn nuisance, I have not time to go the country at this moment, but I suppose I shall have to do what the Duke asks!"

* * *

Thinking of the Earl now, the Duke thought how his party for this week-end had been planned to amuse the Princess Zenka Kozlovski.

She was quite the most attractive woman he had met for a long time.

She was a widow, and she had come to London because she said she was tired of all the pomp and grandeur she had to endure in St. Petersburg.

The Duke had met her at a Dinner Party given by the Duchess of Richmond.

He had been aware as soon as he saw the Princess that she was the most beautiful person he had seen in a long time.

There was also something about her that appealed to his body as well as his eyes.

It was a vibration which seemed in a way to set him alight, to feel an unusually fiery desire even before they talked together.

He was aware as they met that she felt the same.

It was only a question of time before they were involved in a wild love affair that had the gossips whispering the moment they appeared together.

chapter three

As the Duke suggested, Solita went upstairs to lie down.

As she got into bed she realised that she was very tired, and she fell asleep almost at once.

When she awoke it was to hear somebody moving about the room, and found it was the maid, who was preparing her bath.

It took Solita a moment to accustom her eyes to the glamour of the room.

With its painted ceiling, antique inlaid furniture, mirrors surrounded by Cupids, and pictures by master artists, it was a dream of luxury.

The Villa where she had lived in Italy had been beautiful, but in a very different way from the Castle, and certainly not so impressive.

When the maid had finished preparing her bath, Solita stepped into its scented water and thought how lucky she was.

She knew from the very limited amount of money she had left that she would have been able to afford only a small room at a second class Hotel.

Doubtless, too, it would have been on the top floor.

She knew the Duke was being kind; at the same time, she still resented his attitude towards her father's death.

Any real friend, she thought, would have wished to fight back at the Russians, certainly not entertained them in their own home.

She was intelligent enough, however, to realise that the Duke was right in saying that she must be polite as long as they were his guests.

She knew also that she could not start a lone battle with the Russians, without somebody to support her.

At the same time, she swore that she would hate them for the rest of her life.

She would never forgive them for not only killing her father, but so many British soldiers on the North West Frontier.

The maids had unpacked for her, and she fortunately had in her luggage one of her prettiest gowns.

Her "Aunt Mildred," as she called the Duke's Cousin, had been very generous in the way she dressed her.

Miss Leigh had been quite a rich woman, but it had never crossed Solita's mind that when she died her money would all go back to her family.

She had therefore been unable to make any provision for the child she had more or less adopted so generously.

Solita was to learn this from Mildred Leigh's Solicitors in Naples.

They arrived as soon as they learned of her death, and without any warning Solita found she had no home and no money.

She had sat down and considered her position with a good sense that was far beyond her years.

She had been deeply resentful and hurt by the Duke's indifference, but he was the one person who would know what had happened to her father's money.

She felt he must have left some, and the only thing she could do in the circumstances was to go to England to find him.

She had brought away with her everything she possessed, which filled a considerable number of trunks.

Some of them contained books which her adopted Aunt had given her because she knew how much she appreciated them.

They were in fact books in every language, mostly history, and to Solita they were her most treasured possessions.

It hurt her to have to sell her jewellery, but there was nothing else she could do, and what she obtained for it had paid for her fare to England.

She was wise enough to know because she was alone that it would be a mistake to travel anything but First Class.

Although when she arrived in London it left her practically penniless, she had at least, she thought, enough clothes to last her for a long time.

When she learnt that the Duke was at the Castle, she hoped he would allow her to stay for one night, but had never expected or contemplated that it might be longer.

She had asked the Butler at Calver House in Park Lane if she could leave her trunks there until she sent for them.

"That can be quite easily arranged, Miss," he replied.

Solita had therefore taken with her only a small trunk which she knew had been packed with everything she was likely to require.

It was fortunate that it contained a really lovely evening gown.

She had actually packed this particular trunk so that

it could be used for several days in London, or until she found somewhere to live without having to unpack the rest.

As she looked in the mirror she thought the Duke would not be ashamed of her appearance among his smart friends.

The gown was a Paris model. The soft blue silk which matched her eyes had been swept back into a small bustle at the back.

It was decorated round the hem of the skirt with pink roses, and the same flowers adorned the *décolletage* of the bodice, which rested on the edge of her shoulders.

It made her waist look tiny, and gave her an elegance which was unusual in such a young girl.

She went down the Grand Staircase slowly.

She felt as if she had stepped onto the stage of the Opera House and was taking part in one of the elaborate performances which she had seen in Rome.

A footman escorted her across the hall.

He opened the doors of a large Salon in which, Solita realised, many of the Duke's guests had already assembled.

Her eyes were dazzled for a moment by the enormous crystal chandeliers which hung from the ceiling.

She was dazzled, too, by the large amount of jewellery worn by the ladies in their hair, round their necks, and on their arms.

Solita had, however, seen quite a number of well-dressed women when she was staying with her School friends.

In the last year she had even attended some of the parties that her friends' parents gave.

In Naples, too, Mildred Leigh before she became ill, took her to several Balls and Receptions.

She was therefore quite at ease as she walked towards the Duke.

He detached himself from the people to whom he had been talking, and met her halfway down the room.

"You are rested?" he asked.

"Yes, thank you."

He looked at her, she thought critically, so she said:

"I hope, if you are intending to introduce me as your Ward, you will not be ashamed of me!"

"Now you are fishing for compliments. You know as well as I do that you look lovely."

The Duke led her towards his guest and introduced them, noting as he did so that Solita's curtsy was very graceful.

He was prepared for the astonishment of his friends when he told them Solita was his Ward.

"Why have I not heard about Miss Gresham before?" one Lady enquired somewhat querulously.

"Because she returned only this afternoon from Italy, where she has been living," the Duke explained.

They were prevented from asking a great number of additional questions, for at that moment the door opened and the Butler announced:

"The Princess Zenka Kozlovski and Prince Ivan Vlasov."

Solita stiffened.

Because she was so curious, she tried not to stare at the new arrivals.

Then, as the Duke hurried to greet the Princess, Solita saw that without exception she was one of the most beautiful people she had ever seen.

Her hair was dark and swept back from her oval forehead, which made her look different from every other woman in the room, as they were all wearing fashionable fringes.

Her skin was dazzlingly white.

Her eyes, dark and very large, were slightly tilted at the corners, which gave her a mysterious, enigmatic look.

Solita was certain every man would find her both fascinating and intriguing.

She was magnificently dressed in a gown that screamed Paris in every frill and bow, and its small train flowed behind her as she moved over the carpet like a wave of the sea.

Her jewellery was as fantastic as she was herself.

Emeralds glittered against the whiteness of her skin and the small tiara on her head made her look like a Queen.

The Duke kissed her hand and the Princess said in a soft voice which only he could hear:

"It is wonderful to see you again."

"That is what I was intending to say," he replied.

As he looked into her eyes he thought he could see the fire in them.

Without meaning to, his fingers tightened on hers.

Then the Princess said:

"You have not met my brother Ivan, and he has been greatly looking forward to meeting you."

The Prince, as the Duke had expected, was exceedingly handsome in a very Russian way.

His hair was also dark, and his features clear-cut.

His high cheekbones and the darkness of his eyes were very Russian.

"My sister was telling me," he said to the Duke in perfect English, "how kind you have been to her, and I am extremely grateful."

"How could anyone be anything else?" the Duke replied lightly.

He led the Prince and Princess towards his guests and introduced them one by one.

Solita was the last, and when they reached her the Duke said:

"May I present my Ward, Solita Gresham, who has only just arrived in England from the Continent."

"Your Ward?" the Princess questioned. "You have not told me about her before."

"It is a long story," the Duke said hastily, "but, now that she is here, I know she will enjoy herself."

"How could she do anything else when she is with you?" the Princess said.

The look she gave the Duke was very revealing, and Solita, glancing at him, realised how infatuated he was.

It was not surprising, as the Princess was so beautiful.

At the same time, she longed to tell him that it was a mistake to choose a woman with Russian nationality.

Then the Duke was introducing Solita to the Prince.

As she touched his hand she felt almost as if she had a shock.

The Prince was smiling ingratiatingly, and his dark eyes appeared to be complimentary, but she told herself she was not being prejudiced when she knew he was dangerous, so dangerous that she felt as if she were touching a reptile.

"How can the Duke be so foolish," she asked herself, "as to invite these people here?"

Then she was aware that after what he had said to her he would be furious if she did not behave with propriety towards the Prince and the Princess.

"Have you been in England long?" she asked the

48

Prince, knowing it would be a mistake not to appear conversational.

"On this visit only for the last three months," he replied, "but I love England and look upon it as my second home."

As he spoke Solita knew he was lying.

She was not quite sure how she knew, but an instinct which had never betrayed her told her that the Prince did not like England or the English people.

He was, however, talking animatedly to several of the Ladies in the party, who he had met before.

He was paying them compliments which appeared to delight them.

At the same time, he seemed to be on good terms with the Duke's male guests.

They proceeded into dinner, and the Duke took the Princess on his arm. Solita was relieved to find that she was not sitting near either of the Russians.

She was halfway down the table.

Yet she could see through the gold ornaments and the displays of orchids that the Princess behaved very intimately with her host.

She did not touch him, but the way she looked at him, and he looked at her, Solita thought scornfully, they might as well be in each other's arms.

The man on her right was one of the Duke's closest friends.

He was clearly surprised at her sudden appearance, and was extremely curious to know who she was and where she came from.

She told him the truth.

"My father was in the same Regiment as the Duke and saved his life. Then when I was orphaned, His Grace promised to look after me."

"I am absolutely astonished!"

His name, Solita learnt, was Wilfred Denham, but he was known to everybody as "Willy."

"But why?" she asked.

"Because Hugo has never talked about you, and I was in the same Regiment as he was."

"Then perhaps you knew my father?" Solita suggested. "His name was Charles Gresham."

"Of course I knew Charles Gresham!" Willy replied. "And you tell me you are his daughter?"

"I am."

"Then let me say that if there is anything I can do for you—you have only to ask."

"Thank you," Solita said, "but why?"

"Because your father was one of the most charming men I have ever met. He looked after all his young subalterns from the moment they joined the Regiment, and especially when they first came under fire from the enemy. None of us will ever forget him!"

The way Willy spoke was so sincere that Solita felt the tears come into her eyes.

"Thank you, and thank you too for . . . saying you will be . . . my friend. I am very much in need of . . . friends at . . . the moment."

"Why is that?"

"Because for the past ten years I have been living with the Duke's Cousin in Naples, so I know no one in England."

"Looking like you do and being your father's daughter, it is something you will not be able to say in a few months' time," Willy said firmly.

After that, Solita began to enjoy the dinner and the party.

The Gentleman on her other side was slightly older

and was, she discovered, having a very ardent flirtation with the Lady next to him.

He spoke only a few words to Solita, then was drawn away possessively.

Solita was, however, quite content to just look around.

This was her first Dinner Party in England, and she wanted to compare it to those she had seen in other countries.

For years she and the girls with whom she stayed had been too young to come down to dinner.

They had therefore peeped at the guests either from the landing, when they arrived, or through the Minstrels' Gallery, when there was one.

When she was seventeen, she and the daughter of the same age had been allowed to join the guests at dinner, but had to go to bed early.

The Italian parties had been much the same as the Duke's.

Except, Solita thought, his was not so formal as the Italians, nor as animated as the French, who talked across the table.

A number of people joined in the same arguments, their voices rising as they gesticulated with their hands, while the very air vibrated with the violence of their feelings.

Perhaps she had been unlucky, but she had found the Spanish dinner parties were long-drawn-out, and often exceedingly dull.

The parents of the Spanish girl with whom she had made friends were minor Royalty, and she found protocol in Madrid strict and unbending.

Looking round the table now, she thought the Duke looked very regal, but, at the same time, human.

She hated the idea of him being infatuated with the Russian Princess.

She had to be honest and admit, however, that no man could be more handsome or dignified.

It would also be impossible for anyone to look more beautiful than the Princess.

And yet, though Solita knew it was because she was trying to find fault, she thought that the Princess's beauty had something sinister about it.

"I am being imaginative," she told herself, and did not realise she had said the words aloud.

"About what?" Willy enquired, having overheard her.

Solita answered him truthfully.

"I was thinking about the Princess."

"And what did you think about her?"

Solita remembered the Duke's instructions, and she answered:

"She is very beautiful!"

"I agree with you, and she is a complete contrast to the English style of beauty, which is usually described as 'like a rose'!"

Willy spoke in a way which made Solita laugh.

"I hope no one will say that about me!"

"I think it is unlikely," Willy replied, "because even though you are fair and blue-eyed, you are not typically English."

"Why not?"

"It is difficult to explain," he said, "but I think the flower you most resemble is the lily-of-the-valley, or one of those star-shaped orchids at which we are looking now."

He put out his hand as he spoke and picked up one of the orchids which decorated the table.

It was star-shaped and completely white save for two small pink spots on one of its petals.

He held it up against Solita's face and said:

"Yes, I am right, that is what you resemble!"

"I am very flattered," Solita replied, "but I could never aspire to anything so unusual, or so beautiful."

"Now you are being unduly modest," Willy teased, "and I am sure I am right."

He put the orchid down in front of her.

When dinner was over and the Ladies withdrew, Solita picked up the little orchid and carried it with her into the Drawing Room, where they had met before dinner.

She thought as she entered the room that the Ladies, each in a different way, resembled a flower of some sort.

They walked with their bustles moving with every step they took, their diamonds flashing, the exotic fragrance of their different perfumes coming from them.

Solita thought there was no description more apt.

Then, as she looked at the Princess, she thought that despite the fact that she was very lovely, no one could say she resembled a flower.

She was more like a leopardess, beautiful in her own way, feline, graceful, and at the same time dangerous.

"I hate her!" Solita said to herself.

She could see almost as if it were a picture on front of her eyes, her father leading his Platoon through the rocky terrain of the North West Frontier.

The tribesmen had been waiting for them, hiding in the caves, and behind rocks.

They were equipped with Russian weapons, and they were directed by Russian brains.

The British had died from a volley of gunfire from which none of them could escape.

"I hate her!" Solita said again.

Because she found it hard even to look at her, she moved away towards the window.

She pulled aside a damask curtain and looked out.

The stars were filling the sky, and there was a young moon climbing up over the oak trees in the Park.

It was very beautiful, and Solita drew in her breath.

"This is England," she told herself, "and this is where I belong."

Because it was a Friday evening, the party broke up early.

"Tomorrow night," the Duke promised, "I have a special entertainment which I think you will enjoy."

"Oh, Hugo!" one of the ladies exclaimed. "You are always so clever; you always think of something new and original to delight us!"

"That is what I try to do," the Duke replied, "but I have the feeling that it will not be long before I run out of ideas!"

There was a cry of protest to say that was impossible.

Solita noticed that the Princess did not join in.

She was merely looking at the Duke with what she thought was hungry eyes.

'She will devour him!' she thought scornfully. 'Then he will learn too late what a fool he is!'

Then Willy was at her side, asking her if she would like to ride tomorrow morning, and saying that it was what he and the Duke usually did.

The male guests often joined them, but the Ladies nearly always preferred to stay in bed.

"I would like very much to ride," Solita said. "It is something I enjoy more than anything else."

"I had an idea that was what you liked," Willy replied.

"Why?"

"Because your father was a brilliant rider, and I would not expect his daughter to be anything else."

"It is so wonderful for me to be able to talk about Papa," Solita said. "Aunt Mildred, who was the Duke's Cousin with whom I lived, had never met him, nor had anybody else in Italy."

"What I will do," Willy said, "is to find one or two of his friends, and when you go back to London, I will introduce them to you."

Solita gave a deep sigh.

"I would love that, and it is very kind of you to think of me."

"I feel a great many men will be doing that before you are much older!" Willy remarked. "Is Hugo planning to take you to London?"

"He said that his grandmother would chaperon me there."

Willy smiled.

"Well, then, you are in luck! She is the most delightful person and very broadminded. I know you will be happy with her."

He paused, then added as an afterthought:

"Until you are married."

"Why do you say that?" Solita asked.

"Well, it is obvious—looking like you do, there will be a string of suitors for your hand."

"But, I have no wish to be married," Solita protested, "not until I—"

She stopped, realising that what she had been about to say would have been indiscreet, and lapsed into silence.

"What were you going to say?" Willy asked.

"It is something I should not say, so please forget it!"

"I would like you to trust me."

"I do, but occasionally I say things that are very indiscreet, and that would have been one of them."

"Now I am even more curious than I was before," Willy said.

Solita did not answer, and fortunately at that moment somebody came up to speak to him.

She told herself she must be careful, otherwise the Duke would be annoyed.

She knew now, having seen the Princess and her brother, that she was even more determined than she had been before.

Somehow, in some way, she would make the Russians pay for her father's death and the treacherous manner in which it had happened.

'I hate them, I hate them!' she was thinking as she said goodnight.

The Princess had given her only a cursory nod, as if she were of no consequence, but Prince Ivan had said:

"I have been unlucky this evening, Miss Gresham, in not having the chance to talk to you. Perhaps tomorrow the gods, or rather you, will favour me!"

He held out his hand as he spoke, but Solita pretended not to see it.

Instead, she curtsied and murmured, "You are very kind," and moved hastily away from him.

As she said goodnight to the Duke he said:

"Sleep well, Solita, and tomorrow I want to show you over the Castle."

"That will be very exciting!" Solita replied. "And thank you very much for everything."

He smiled at her and she walked upstairs behind two of the other Ladies, wishing she could warn him not to become too involved with the Princess.

She realised, however, that if she said anything against her, the Duke would undoubtedly defend her hotly.

He would also be annoyed at her for again expressing her hatred of the Russians.

The maid, who had looked after her earlier in the evening, was waiting in her bedroom.

She helped Solita out of her gown and hung it up in the wardrobe.

"You looked lovely tonight, Miss, an' they was sayin' downstairs as you're th' prettiest young lady as evers come to th' Castle!"

"Thank you," Solita said, "but I cannot compete with beauties like the Princess!"

"Oh, her!" the maid said. "She's beautiful, all right, but as 'ard as nails!"

Although Solita knew it was not correct to discuss such things with the servants, she could not help asking:

"What makes you say that?"

"It's the way she behaved with her lady's-maid, Miss. She's French, an' ever so nice, but she 'as an awful time with the Princess. Orders 'er about, she does, as if she's dirt beneath her feet!"

The maid sighed.

"Them Russians be all the same—treats those beneath them as if they was serfs!"

Solita was not surprised.

She had read about the serfs and the cruelty they incurred from their masters.

She knew it was something that would not be tolerated in England.

The maid, whose name was Emily, put away her satin slippers and tidied the room. Then she blew out the candles, leaving only one burning by the bed.

"Is there anythin' else you wants, Miss?" she asked.

"No thank you," Solita replied. "What time does His Lordship go riding in the morning?"

"Seven o'clock, Miss—he goes out early!"

"I will be riding with him and Mr. Denham," Solita said, "so please call me at six-thirty."

"You'll not be too tired, Miss?"

"No! I am used to getting up early," Solita replied.

"Then I'll call you prompt, an' bring you some tea."

Emily opened the door.

"Sleep well, Miss, an' the Angels watch over you, as me mother used t'say."

Alone, Solita snuggled down in bed.

She expected to fall asleep immediately, then she realised she was missing the book she always read before she went to sleep.

She looked around the room, and realised that there could not have been a book in the trunk she had brought with her.

Then she remembered when she had first come upstairs to rest that the Housekeeper had told her there was a Boudoir connected with her bedroom.

She had been too tired to explore it then.

Now she told herself there would certainly be a book she could read for perhaps twenty minutes which would send her off to sleep.

She got out of bed and found the communicating door near to the window.

She turned the handle, but it was locked. Then she saw that the key was still in the lock.

She opened the door and found, as she expected, a very elegantly furnished room.

It was lit by two oil lamps, and she guessed they

were safer than candles if they were to be left burning all night.

There were vases filled with hot-house carnations on several small tables beside a comfortable sofa and arm-chairs. Also there were a number of small silver and gold objects.

At the end of the room Solita saw what she was seeking: a Chippendale bookcase.

She hurried across the thick carpet in her bare feet and looked with delight at the books.

They were in English and there were several she had already read. One or two others she had heard of and was sure she would find them interesting.

She was pulling them out and deciding which she would take back to bed with her when she heard a voice speaking.

She realised with a start it was in Russian.

For a moment she thought she must be dreaming, until she saw that at the side of the bookcase there was another door.

It was slightly ajar, and there was just a sliver of light coming through it from the other side.

"What did you find out?" she heard a man's voice ask, and knew it was Prince Ivan speaking.

"Very little, except that his father coded the message that went last night."

Now the Princess was speaking.

Without realising she was doing so, Solita moved a little closer to the door that was ajar.

"What I have come to tell you," Prince Ivan said, "is that when you are with our host tonight, you must find out from him why he was at the India Office."

"The India Office?" Princess Zenka exclaimed.

"I heard him tell one of the men at dinner that Kimberley is giving away the prizes at the Horse Show which is taking place in a fortnight's time."

"Why should you think he had any other reason for going there?" the Princess enquired.

Prince Ivan was silent for a moment before he replied:

"I did not tell you, but I heard a rumour which I have not yet been able to substantiate that the Duke was in Finland last year."

"In Finland?" the Princess echoed. "Do you mean when the explosion took place?"

"I cannot be sure," Prince Ivan replied, "and, naturally, it would be no use asking him openly, so you will have to find out by hypnotism."

There was silence while Solita held her breath.

Then the Princess answered:

"It would be best to do it when he is asleep, but it is not so easy that way, as you well know."

"Asleep or awake," the Prince said sharply, "If you find out that the Duke was involved, it will be a distinct 'feather in our caps.'"

"Yes, of course," the Princess agreed, "but I do not think for one moment that he is any different from the usual Englishman, who thinks only of horses—and, of course, women!"

"He is certainly infatuated with you," Prince Ivan said, "so keep him that way. He might come in useful!"

"I shall do my best," the Princess exclaimed, "and he is certainly a change from that dreadful old German!"

"There I agree with you," Prince Ivan remarked, "and if I have to eat sauerkraut ever again, I swear I shall resign!"

"You will not be allowed to do that," the Princess

answered, "you are in too deep, and you know that General Tcherevin is delighted with you."

"So he damned well ought to be!" Prince Ivan laughed. "We have given them information that no one else could have obtained."

He laughed again, and it was a very unpleasant sound.

"Do you know how many British soldiers were ambushed last month?"

"I do not know, and I do not care!" the Princess snapped. "But now you had better go back to your room. It would be a mistake for the Duke to find you here with me."

"Yes, you are right," Prince Ivan agreed. "Goodnight, my dear, and find out everything you can, after, of course, you have enjoyed yourself!"

"I shall certainly do that," the Princess replied.

Prince Ivan was obviously leaving the bedroom, and Solita became aware of her own position.

Swiftly, making no sound with her bare feet, she slipped across the Boudoir and into her own room.

Carefully, so as not to make any noise, she closed the communicating door.

As she put down the book she held she thought she must be dreaming.

Now she knew the truth!

The Princess and her brother were spies—spies for the Russian Third Section.

They were responsible for the deaths of innumerable British soldiers.

Spies. And the way they did it was to hypnotise the information out of their victims!

It was then, as she stood there, that she realised she had gone to the wrong Boudoir.

The one in which she had just been eavesdropping was connected to the Princess's room.

Opposite her was a door into the Boudoir which included the Queen Henrietta Maria Suite.

It was immaterial, and it would have been a quite easy mistake to make.

But she understood now why the key, forgotten by a careless housemaid, was still in the lock.

It suddenly swept over her even more forcefully than when she had first heard it what the Princess intended to do.

When the Duke was with her, as he would be in a very short while, she intended to hypnotise him into finding out where he had been in Finland, and why he had been at the India Office yesterday.

Solita could not believe for one moment that there was anything sinister to be discovered.

But the idea of the Duke being at the mercy of a Russian made every nerve in her body revolt.

It was degrading and humiliating that the Duke, even though he had hurt her, should be at the mercy of the Russians who had killed her father.

'I have to save him,' she thought.

It flashed through her mind that Prince Ivan had implied that the Duke would be going to the Princess's room to make love to her.

The idea shocked Solita.

She told herself if he suffered through associating with a Russian, it would be his own fault.

Then she knew in some obscure way she did not understand that British lives were in danger.

'I have to warn him,' she thought.

She looked around the room as if asking for help.

Then she was aware as she saw herself reflected in

the mirror that she was wearing only her nightgown.

Impatiently she slipped on the negligee which went over it which had been laid out by Emily on a chair.

Then she opened the door which led out into the corridor.

She opened it very, very softly, afraid there might be somebody outside, somebody who would think it strange that she was coming out of her bedroom so late at night.

She knew the Duke slept at the end of the corridor.

The Housekeeper had mentioned it when Solita had exclaimed at how beautiful her bedroom was.

"It's one of the State Rooms, Miss, which are used by all His Grace's personal friends," she said. "We always calls it 'The Royal Passage' amongst ourselves."

"I am sure that is the right word for it," Solita had replied with a smile.

"His Grace's Suite is at the end," the Housekeeper informed her, "and that's got portraits of several of the Kings who have stayed at the Castle."

She spoke proudly and went on:

"Next to that is 'Queen Elizabeth's Suite', and you, Miss, are in the Suite called after Queen Henrietta Maria, wife of Charles II."

"It makes me feel very grand!" Solita smiled.

"I think it's one of the prettiest," the Housekeeper said, "and you're just the right person to be in it, Miss."

Solita had been pleased at the compliment, but what was important was that she now knew where the Duke was sleeping.

She also knew why the Princesss was in the "Queen Elizabeth Suite" next door.

Her heart was pounding because she was afraid that Prince Ivan would be in the corridor.

Some of the lights in the silver sconces had been extinguished, but it was easy to see her way to the double doors at the end.

She thought she would make less sound if she went barefooted, and she ran on tiptoe past the Princess's Suite and reached the Duke's.

She had the feeling there was little time to spare before he visited the Princess, and she might be too late.

She turned the handle of the door, and when it opened slipped through it as if she were a ghost.

She was not, however, in a bedroom, but in a small *entre-salle*.

It had three candles to light it and she could see quite clearly a door opposite which she was sure was the Duke's bedroom.

For a moment she hesitated, afraid she might hear voices and that his Valet was with him.

Then, as there was only silence, she took a deep breath and turned the handle of the bedroom door.

chapter four

As Solita entered the room she saw it was very large and there was a huge four-poster facing her.

The light came from candelabra on each side of it.

With a sudden jerk of her heart she realised that the bed was empty.

That meant, she thought, that the Duke had already gone to the Princess.

Then, as she stood irresolute, looking at the bed as if she felt she must be mistaken, a door opened and the Duke came in.

For a moment he was silhouetted against the light behind him, and she saw that he was wearing a long dark robe.

He did not see her, but walked across the room and she knew that he was on his way to the Princess.

Suddenly he was aware of her, standing just inside the door, and looked at her in sheer astonishment.

"Solita!" he exclaimed. "Why are you here?"

She shut the door behind her, then said in a low voice:

"The Princess is going to hypnotise you!"

The Duke stared at her and she added:

"She wants to find out why you were at the India Office, and—"

"What the devil are you talking about?" the Duke interrupted. "Really, Solita, your imagination, or, rather, your hatred of the Russians, is no longer a joke!"

He spoke angrily; Solita turned back towards the door.

She was actually turning the handle when the Duke said:

"Wait!"

She wanted to disobey him; she wanted to leave him to his plight.

If he was really so foolish as to be infatuated with a Russian, then he deserved to suffer for it.

Then Solita remembered her father's death at their hands.

She did not turn around, she only waited, and the Duke said in a different tone of voice:

"Tell me again what you have just said. I did not mean to be rude, but you surprised me."

"I was warning you," Solita said in a very low voice, "that the Princess says she intends to hypnotise you."

"She said? To whom? To you?"

Again there was an incredulous note in his voice and he was so obviously irritated that Solita wanted to leave him.

Once again she turned the handle, and as if he realised that she really intended to go, the Duke said:

"For God's sake, Solita, be reasonable! You can hardly expect me to believe what you are saying if you do not explain further."

"What is . . . the point . . . if you think I am . . . lying?"

"I think nothing of the sort!" the Duke said. "Turn round and tell me exactly what you came to say."

Reluctantly, her eyes very large in her pale face, Solita turned round.

For a moment she almost doubted what she had heard.

It seemed impossible in this imposing English Castle that Russian spies should have ingratiated themselves into the Duke's affections.

He called them his friends.

Yet she had known from the first moment she met the Princess and Prince Ivan that they were dangerous.

Because she was nervous, she clasped her hands together and stood looking up at the Duke questioningly.

She looked small, frail, and very young.

It flashed through his mind that she was just an imaginative child playing a game to try to scare him.

With a faint smile he said:

"Tell me the truth, and I will listen to what you have to say without interrupting."

In a small voice, but he could hear her clearly, Solita said:

"I . . . I went by mistake into . . . the Boudoir adjoining . . . the Princess's bedroom . . . thinking it was . . . mine."

"The door should have been locked!" the Duke said.

"It was, but the key was there."

The Duke frowned, and Solita went on:

"I . . . I was just selecting a book when I heard two people speaking in Russian."

"You understand Russian?"

"Yes, yes! I am quite fluent in that language."

"So you knew what they were saying."

"Prince Ivan spoke first. He said: 'What have you found out?'

"The Princess replied:

67

"'Very little, except that his father coded the message himself that went . . .'"

"Did she say—'his father'?" the Duke interrupted.

"Yes."

"You are quite certain?"

"I can remember the actual words," and she repeated:

"'Very little, except that his father coded the message himself that went last night.'"

The Duke drew in his breath and put his hand up to his forehead.

Then in a rather strange tone he said:

"What happened after that?"

Solita looked at him apprehensively as she said:

"I moved a little . . . closer to the door which was . . . slightly ajar, and I head Prince Ivan saying:

"'What I came to tell you is that when you are with our host tonight, you must find out from him why he was at the India Office.'"

"You are quite sure he said that?" the Duke asked.

"Absolutely, and the Princess seemed surprised."

"Go on," the Duke said again.

Solita told him what Prince Ivan had said about Lord Kimberley giving away the prizes at the Horse Show.

Then, looking at the Duke questioningly, she told him what the Prince had added.

"'I heard a rumour which I have not yet been able to substantiate that the Duke was in Finland last year.'"

"He said 'Finland'?" the Duke questioned.

"Yes, and the Princess answered:

"'It would be best to do it when he is asleep, but as you know, it is not as easy that way.'"

The Duke gave an exclamation which Solita thought was one of incredulity.

Speaking quickly, because she wanted to get it over

with, she related that she had heard the Princess say: "He was a change from 'the old German.'"

She thought it sounded rude and therefore looked away from the Duke as she continued.

She told him how Prince Ivan had said that if he had to eat sauerkraut again he would resign.

"The Princess replied to that," she went on, "that he was in too deep, and that General Tcherevin was delighted with him."

Then she looked at the Duke to say in a tone that was accusing:

"General Tcherevin is the Head of the Russian Secret Police."

"I know that," the Duke said sharply. "Go on!"

Solita hesitated, as if she could hardly find words to say what was in her mind. Then in a voice that was one of undoubted horror she said:

"Prince Ivan laughed and asked:

"'Do you know how many British soldiers were ambushed last month?'"

"You are making it up!" the Duke exclaimed. "I do not believe for a moment that Prince Ivan or any other man would say such a thing!"

His anger took Solita by surprise and her eyes seemed to grow larger than they were already.

Then they seemed to blaze at the Duke.

"I swear before God and on my father's grave," she said, "that every word I have told you is the truth as I heard it!"

She glared at the Duke as she went on:

"If the Princess means . . . more to you than the . . . lives of your own countrymen, then there is . . . nothing I can do . . . about it!"

She turned as she spoke and ran across the room.

Before the Duke could stop her she had opened the door and disappeared.

She heard him call out "Solita!" But as he did so she shut the outer door and ran down the empty corridor to her own bedroom.

Once inside, she locked the door, although she was certain the Duke would not follow her.

She sat shaking with anger before she flung off her negligee and got into bed.

"I hate him! I hate him!" she said over and over again. "Tomorrow I will leave and never speak to him again!"

Then, because of what she had overheard, and her encounter with the Duke had been so disturbing, she felt the tears trickle down her cheeks.

She hid her face in her pillow.

When Solita had left, the Duke, standing in the centre of his bedroom, felt his anger ebbing away.

He began to realise that what she had told him was indeed the truth.

It was difficult to credit that the woman he had found so alluring was in reality an accomplished agent of the Russian Secret Police.

She had continually professed herself to be wildly in love with him.

Now that he could think calmly, his acute brain told him it would have been impossible for Solita to have invented that he had been in Finland.

She also could not have known that Lord Kimberley himself decoded the messages he sent to India.

It was then he realised that she had uncovered a plot that had never entered his mind, or Lord Kimberley's.

How could they imagine that the Princess used hypnotism to obtain the information she required.

He remembered now that he had heard that his friend John Wodehouse was an extremely proficient duellist.

He also knew there was an expert on the Russian Ambassador's staff.

It was something which was common knowledge but he had not thought of it until this moment.

He realised it would be a reason for John to go to the Russian Embassy, and, of course, meet the Princess.

He suspected that Prince Ivan was also good at fencing, as a great many Russians were.

It would have been easy for Prince Ivan to persuade John Wodehouse to have a game with him and for the Princess to join them afterwards.

Then she would find a way of hypnotising him, with John not realising for one moment what was happening to him.

It would be quite easy when he returned to London to find out if John had been to the Russian Embassy the previous afternoon, although he knew without investigation what the answer would be.

Then there was the question of his visit to Finland.

He had been so certain that anyone who learnt of his visit would accept his explanation that he had gone salmon fishing.

It was a sport he enjoyed, both in Scotland, and in one year, in Norway.

It had therefore been an excellent excuse if anyone was curious as to why he had been in Finland.

He might have guessed, he thought bitterly, that the Russian Secret Police were more perceptive than he had given them credit as being.

It all passed through his mind very quickly, and he knew how appalling Solita's revelation was.

But he must, unless he wished to arouse the Princess's suspicions, go to her bedroom, where she would be waiting for him.

For a moment, every instinct within him cried out in disgust that she should have tricked him so cleverly.

Then some cool, calculating part of his brain warned him that this was only the beginning.

He had promised the Secretary of State for India that he would help him.

He had to save the men who were being ambushed by an enemy who knew in advance what their orders were.

That was what he had to do now, and he was much better equipped for the task than he had been before.

In fact he knew the first chapter of the drama.

Lord Kimberley had told his son that he himself deciphered the messages that went by Morse Code to India.

They travelled via the Submarine Cable which went from the Foreign Office to the Viceroy in Calcutta.

It was very unlikely, in fact the Princess had not said so, that John knew what the message was.

He was aware only that because it was so secret, his father did it himself.

What the Duke knew he had to find out was how, when the code reached India, it was transmitted to the Russians before the British obeyed their orders.

As he thought it out, the Duke ceased to be the charming, genial host he had been at dinner, an Englishman concerned only with the comfort of his guests, a man who was more interested in his horses and estates than anything else.

Instead, he became a soldier who had taken part in what the British referred to as "The Great Game."

That was the most efficient and brilliantly performed Secret Service operation in the world.

It was the Duke's tremendous self-control, and the way his instinct helped and guided him, which had made him successful in the projects he had undertaken in the past.

They had all been exceedingly dangerous.

Almost on every occasion he had been within a hair's-breadth of losing his life, or of being exposed.

It was through sheer ability that he had been victorious.

Although few people were aware of it, he had earned an award for gallantry half-a-dozen times over.

He had never, however, been given a medal, because in "The Great Game" no one was rewarded.

In fact, for safety's sake, none of the participants were known to each other.

They were just numbers, and even to the heads of the Regiments with whom he was involved, Hugo Leigh had been just "Number 29."

Now the Duke, as if he had been called to attention by a Senior Officer, walked towards the door.

He knew he had to act the part that was expected of him.

Only by using an iron control over himself and his feelings, as he had used them in the past, would he be able to allay any suspicion the Princess might harbour about him.

He thought, however, what he would do if he could behave as he wished.

It would give him the greatest pleasure to put his hands round the Princess's long white throat and throttle a confession out of her.

But that would be a stupid thing to do.

There would still be Prince Ivan to deal with, and the Russian Secret Police.

They would immediately be aware that their suspicions, as yet unverified, were true.

He therefore let himself out of his bedroom and walked slowly and purposefully the short distance to the Queen Elizabeth room.

He opened the door. . . .

*　*　*

Nearly two hours later, the Duke with his eyes shut was breathing evenly.

In the faint light coming from the candles which the Princess had left burning behind the diaphanous curtains of the bed, he looked sound asleep.

Very gently the Princess raised her head.

With her long, dark silky hair flowing over her white shoulders, she was in the half-light very lovely.

There was a faint smile on her lips.

Never in her long experience of lovers of every nationality had she ever known one more handsome or more ardent.

Slowly, moving as sensuously as a snake, she sat up in bed so that she could look down on the sleeping Duke.

He was utterly relaxed.

Again moving very slowly, she slipped one hand behind his neck, and the fingers of the other, light as a feather, moved over his forehead.

"Sleep . . ." she whispered, "Sleep . . ."

He did not move, nor did his eyes flicker.

After a moment she said in a voice that was little above a whisper:

"You are asleep, Hugo! You are dreaming . . . and

you are dreaming of Finland . . . the land you visited last year . . . tell me . . . what do you see . . . what are you dreaming . . . ?"

The Duke did not move, and after a moment she said again:

"Where are you, Hugo? Where are you at this moment?"

"In—Finland!"

The Duke's voice was low and almost inarticulate.

"And what are you doing? What are you doing in Finland?"

"Fi-shing."

"And what else? Do you see a gun?"

There was silence, and after a moment the Princess asked again:

"Do you see a big gun?"

"Salmon," the Duke murmured, "many—salmon—very good—catch!"

The Princess's fingers moved again over his forehead and the hand at the back of his neck tightened a little.

"Now you are in the India Office, Hugo . . . why did you go there?"

Again there was silence before the Duke replied slowly:

"Ask—Kimberley—Horse Show."

The Princess's lips tightened, then she said:

"Do you know about the secret messages to India? Did Lord Kimberley tell you about them?"

There was a long pause.

"Tell me," she insisted, "tell me what you learnt at the India Office."

"Horses," the Duke murmured, "get—leaflets printed—quickly."

The Princess gave an exasperated little sigh, then she said:

"When you wake you will remember nothing of this conversation, do you hear? You will remember nothing!"

She looked at him with her green eyes which had been on his face ever since she started her interrogation.

The Duke could feel the power of the vibrations she had been attempting to exercise over him.

He had been aware from the moment she had started that she was extremely experienced.

Unless he was very careful, he would, like so many other men before him, be hypnotised into saying what she wanted to hear.

Years ago, when he first entered "The Great Game," he had been taught by an expert how to avoid being used in such a manner.

He was aware of the Princess's fingers behind his neck holding him in a vise.

He knew, too, that he would, if he listened to her without protecting himself, give the truthful answers to her questions.

His brain would thicken and darken to every beat of his pulse.

Then he would be completely within her power.

The only protection was to concentrate his whole mind on something else, to divorce himself from what was happening.

There was no other way to combat her powers except through the strength of his mind.

His Instructor had said to him:

"Think of anything, focus your attention on it—the Alphabet, the multiplication tables, anything, so long as it prevents your being subjected to the will of the person who is interrogating you."

At first, the Duke had found it a difficult thing to do.

Now, the moment he felt the touch of the Princess's hand on his head, he began to recite a poem to himself which he always enjoyed:

In Xanadu did Kubla Khan
A stately Pleasure-Dome decree . . .

He went all through it, stopping only to answer her questions when her hypnotic powers were relaxed.

He was in no danger until he had finished speaking.

Then he continued with his poem until he knew that finally she had given up and decided he was, as Solita told him she said: "No different from the usual Englishman who thinks only of horses and, of course, women!"

"That is what she now thinks I am!" the Duke told himself triumphantly.

He waited until the Princess had lain down beside him again, then he opened his eyes and yawned.

"Have I been asleep?" he asked. "How very remiss of me, when I might have been kissing you!"

"It is not surprising you are tired," the Princess said gently, "I too am fatigued by the thrill of your love."

"Then I must leave you," the Duke said.

There was a very convincing note of reluctance in his voice, and the Princess said:

"There is always tomorrow, my wonderful, handsome Hugo!"

"As you say," the Duke replied, "there is always tomorrow, and a great many days after it."

He kissed her lightly and rose from the bed.

He was aware as she watched him putting on his robe that she was disappointed.

It was, he thought, where she was concerned, the failure of omission, but for him so far, a success!

It was three o'clock in the morning when he returned to his own room, but he was in fact not tired.

He was thinking of how he must communicate with Lord Kimberley as quickly as possible, and they must decide what was to be done next.

As he got into bed he was thinking that really Kimberley could do very little except in the future prevent his son from going to the Russian Embassy.

Solita had shown him where the fault lay in England.

He had still to find out how the Russians received the messages sent from the India Office before they could be imparted to the British soldiers concerned.

Now, in his own comfortable bed, the Duke went over the position as it was at the moment.

The British had invented Submarine Cables and they had at first taken a route which had involved crossing Germany, Russia, Teheran, then on to India.

This was of course a very vulnerable route and the next was also unsatisfactory.

It ran across Europe to Constantinople, across Turkey, to the Persian Gulf, and from there to Karachi.

Twelve years before, a much better route had been opened via Gibraltar, Malta, Alexandria, Suez, and Aden to Bombay.

This belonged to the English Telegraph Company, but was carried from Bombay overland to Calcutta by the Indian Telegraph Company.

It was a very long distance, and there were many hazards and difficulties.

The Duke knew that the Russians were waiting to take advantage any way they could find.

What would be important for them was to know which of the thousands of messages sent by Morse Code were the ones from the India Office in London.

This was of course simplified to a great degree if they knew the actual time and date a message was being sent by the Secretary of State.

This message would go in Diplomatic Code to Calcutta, to the Viceroy.

He therefore worked out that the next step was to discover, when it had reached Calcutta, who intercepted it then gave the information it contained to the Russians.

The Duke turned it over in his mind.

He knew it would be a great mistake for the Princess to have the least suspicion that he had discovered, or rather Solita had, that she and her brother were working for the Secret Police.

Also he was aware it would be disastrous for him to change in any way his attitude towards her.

He had to convince her he was just as infatuated with her as he had been before.

The Duke had dedicated himself when he was a very young man to working both mentally and physically for his country.

He also abhorred the Secret War instigated by the Russians, which had cost so many lives.

The Tsar, Nicholas I, had continually declared his country's friendship for England.

But the fact was that they attempted to "pull the wool over the eyes" of a people they arrogantly believed to be stupid.

"I will make them suffer for this in one way or another!" the Duke swore.

He knew as his feelings welled up inside him that he actively hated the Russians in the same way Solita did.

He was furious with himself because he had been beguiled by the Princess's beauty.

He had also been deceived by her and her brother's continued assertions that they loved England and the English people.

"I have been a fool!" the Duke admitted.

He knew now that somehow, in some way, he would not only prevent the Russians' plan to intercept the cables, he would also manage to expose the Princess.

After that she would be unable to continue her nefarious plots, not only in England, but in other countries as well.

Before he fell asleep he told himself that Solita had saved him.

He might easily tonight have been hypnotised into betraying secrets which would have far-reaching effects.

When morning came he would not have the slightest idea of the damage he had done.

Hypnotism was, he knew, one of the most insidious and clever ways of interrogation, but he had never expected it would be used in England.

In India, it was fairly common, but the hypnotists themselves were usually *Yogis* or *Fakirs*, and not politically minded.

What the Duke now realised was that the Princess had a far more complex character than he might have suspected.

She had also been very skilfully prepared for her role by masterminds in the Russian Secret Service.

It was well known how efficient this was, and how Russian Agents moved in all the European countries seeking out information that might prove of interest to the Tsar.

The Secret Police were feared and actually terrorised a great majority of its people. It was, and still is, part of the Russian genre.

If Tcherevin could not learn what he wanted by more accepted stringent methods, he tortured his victims in such an appalling manner that few of them did not succumb.

The Duke was suddenly aware that if Solita had not discovered the truth about the Princess and her brother, he would at this moment be a marked man.

He also knew that his life, if not in England, then in any other part of the world, would not be worth more than a few pence.

He now realised that Solita was also in danger.

If, by the flicker of an eyelid, she let the Princess or Prince Ivan think she had overheard what had been said in what they believed was a language unlikely to be understood in England, she would be dealt with.

She would either have an unfortunate accident, or suffer some injury that would permanently affect her brain.

"I must warn her," the Duke told himself.

He was thinking the same thing when he rose the next morning.

*   *   *

The Duke's Valet called him at six-thirty.

When Willy informed him that Solita was riding with them, he doubted, after his behaviour last night, that she would join them.

He entered the stable to choose the horse he would

ride, and there was a long array of them waiting in their stalls.

To his surprise, he found Solita already there.

She was talking to his Head Groom and patting as she did so a magnificent stallion which was a new acquisition.

"Good morning, Solita!" the Duke said.

She started, then turned round to look at him.

He thought she looked paler than she had been yesterday and perhaps she had lain awake last night worrying about him.

There was also, he saw, a question in her eyes.

He knew she was wondering whether, after all she had said, he had gone confidently to the Princess and been hypnotised without being aware of it.

"Is this the horse you want to ride?" the Duke enquired.

"If you will permit me to do so," Solita answered.

"Jupiter, as I have rechristened him," the Duke said, "is quite a handful, but I expect you will be able to manage him."

"As I think that is a compliment, I accept with pleasure!" Solita said.

There was a touch of sarcasm in her voice that the Duke did not miss.

"I will ride Pegasus," he said to the groom. "Saddle both horses quickly."

"O' course, Your Grace," the Head Groom replied.

"I suggest we wait outside in the sunshine," the Duke said to Solita.

He walked ahead of her out of the stables into the cobbled yard.

As she joined him, he thought a little reluctantly, he said:

"Everything is all right, and later I will tell you about it."

"Can you be certain of . . . that?" Solita questioned in a low voice.

He knew she was thinking that he had gone to the Princess disbelieving her, and if he had been hypnotised, he would not be aware of it.

"What you suspected happened," he said, "but as you prepared me, no damage has been done."

Solita stared at him, and he saw the sudden light in her eyes.

"You are sure?" she asked.

"Quite sure," he replied, "and I am very much in your debt."

He saw then her whole face light up. It seemed to him touching that she should mind so much.

Then Willy joined them, and there was no chance of saying any more.

They rode through the Park, along some flat land on which they could gallop.

The Duke was aware that Solita was not only perfectly capable of handling Jupiter, but she was also an exceptionally good rider.

It was something he had not expected when he had first seen her.

Then he remembered, as Willy had, that her father had been an outstanding horseman, and it was what he might have expected.

Because she had been living in Italy, he had somehow connected her more with Italian interests and not those that were peculiarly English.

Then she took high jumps as well as he and Willy could do.

She also raced with them across the fields, and there

was little to choose between the speed of the three horses.

He told himself that Solita was very different from most women he knew.

Many of those with whom he had engaged himself recently rode well, and a number of them hunted, but there was something definitely different about the way Solita rode.

It told him that she had an affinity with her horse that was rare.

He saw that she talked to her horse.

She bent forward after they had jumped a high fence to tell Jupiter how well he had done.

By the time they rode back to the Castle, Willy was paying Solita expansive compliments and she was no longer so pale.

Her cheeks were flushed from the exercise.

The Duke knew from the way her eyes were shining and the happiness in her smile that there was another reason besides riding for her elation.

He thought it extraordinarily touching in a girl of her age.

She should be thinking of her beauty and the Social World, in which she would undoubtedly shine, instead of minding so intensely about what was happening in India.

When they returned to the Castle it was still early.

They breakfasted alone, although the Gentlemen were expected downstairs by nine o'clock.

Before they had finished, the Duke was aware that Solita was looking at him pleadingly.

"You will find the newspapers in the Morning Room," he said to Willy. "I have something to say to Solita in my Study, and I will join you later."

"Very well," Willy replied, "but remember, I want to know what your plans are for today. If it is a question of being paired off with one of your guests, my choice is Solita!"

"I will think about it," the Duke replied enigmatically.

He walked towards the Study with Solita at his side.

He shut the door of the Study behind them, then as if she could wait no longer, Solita asked:

"It really was all right . . . and you do not think she . . . hypnotised you while you were . . . asleep?"

She spoke in a low voice, as if she were afraid of being overheard.

The Duke walked to the fireplace before he replied:

"You were quite right, Solita. She tried, but she failed!"

Solita gave a little cry of relief.

"I was afraid, terribly afraid," she said, "and I prayed that you would believe me."

"I did believe you," the Duke said. "You must forgive me for seeming incredulous, but it was something I did not expect—in England!"

He saw the expression on Solita's face and said:

"Do not rub it in! I realise I was wrong to trust a Russian, and I promise you it is something that will not happen again!"

He paused. Then he said:

"At the same time, we have to be very careful, you and I."

She looked up at him in surprise, and he explained:

"Now we know, thanks to you, that the Princess and her brother are spying on behalf of the Secret Police, and you realise that not only my life but also yours is in danger?"

85

Solita looked at him in surprise. Then she said:

"I am not important . . . but you are!"

"We are both important to ourselves and to each other," the Duke replied, "and you are intelligent enough to know that if they had any idea we had discovered their secret, we may both of us be quietly eliminated."

Solita would have given a little cry of fear, but she stifled it with her hand on her lips.

"You must be very, very . . . careful," she said.

"And so must you," the Duke answered. "That is why, Solita, you have to act as you have never acted before, until the Princess and Prince Ivan leave the Castle as we will do."

Solita raised her eyebrows.

"As we will do?" she repeated.

"I have the idea, and it has only just come to me," the Duke said quickly, "that before you start to enjoy the London Season with my grandmother, you are begging me, and I have agreed, to take you to India to visit your father's grave!"

chapter five

SOLITA'S face, the Duke thought, was radiant.

He looked at her for a long moment before he said:

"For God's sake, be careful! If you look as you do now, it would make anyone suspicious that you had been given the Keys to Heaven!"

"That is exactly what you have given me," Solita replied, "and the idea of going to India is the most thrilling thing that has ever happened!"

"We shall have to plan it very carefully," the Duke said. "In the meantime, today is Saturday, and the Russians will not think of leaving until Monday, at the earliest."

Solita looked worried.

"S-suppose she . . . tries again . . . tonight?" she suggested hesitatingly.

"I have already thought of that," the Duke replied. "Leave everything to me, but be prepared if the worse comes to the worst, to leave without any warning."

Solita looked at him in a bewildered fashion, and he said quickly:

"It is always a great mistake to do things in too much of a hurry."

"I know that," Solita replied, "at the same time . . ."

The Duke put his fingers to his lips.

"Remember, you saved me by eavesdropping," he said. "If you can do it, other people can do the same."

"Yes . . . yes, of course," Solita agreed.

She felt as if the Russians were encroaching on them and lurking behind every curtain and piece of furniture.

The Duke smiled at her and said:

"Now we start, both of us, showing our intelligence by concealing it!"

Solita gave a nervous little laugh.

"The more we do and the less we say the better," the Duke said. "At the same time, thank you, Solita, for saving my life as well as many other people's."

As he spoke he raised her hand to his lips and kissed it.

She drew in her breath because she was so surprised, for at the touch of his lips she felt a strange sensation she had never felt before.

"Now that is settled," the Duke said in a different tone of voice, "and we will go and tell Willy our plans for today."

He opened the door as he spoke and they walked side by side down the passage to the Morning Room, where Willy was sitting reading *The Times*.

"Have you finished?" he asked as they walked in. "Several of your guests, Hugo, have come down to breakfast, if you want to see them."

"For the moment I want to talk to you," the Duke said, "and plan how we shall spend the day."

As the two men sat discussing it, Solita was aware that the Duke was making it very difficult for the Princess or any other woman to have a *tête-à-tête* with him.

With Willy's help they planned a picnic luncheon at the famous Folly which had been erected by one of his ancestors.

Then a visit to the hot-houses, which Solita learnt for the first time were famous for their special orchids.

Then, if there was time, those who were not too tired would ride late in the afternoon over the Duke's private Racecourse.

"Please may I do that?" Solita asked, speaking for the first time.

"Of course, if you want to," the Duke replied, "but I think you should have a rest before dinner. On Saturday night we are traditionally late."

It flashed through her mind that if that was so, the Princess would not expect him to go to her bedroom.

Then she had the uncomfortable feeling that the Princess would have very strong ideas about what she wanted.

It would not be easy for the Duke to escape her.

"Supposing she tries again," Solita said to herself, "and this time the Duke is unable to prevent her learning his secrets?"

She felt herself tremble at what this involved.

As if what she was feeling communicated itself to the Duke, he turned his head to say:

"I think, Solita, you should go and change. We shall be driving to the Folly, and I hope you will accompany me, and I also intend to ask Georgina Dudley to travel in my new Phaeton."

"Which is surely meant for two people!" Willy remarked dryly. "I wonder who is chaperoning who?"

"We are all slim enough not to feel crushed," the Duke replied firmly. "Who do you want with you, Willy?"

"I suppose, unless you want her to tear out Solita's hair," Willy said, "I had better escort the Princess!"

"That is what I was about to suggest to you," the Duke said.

"Thank you for nothing!" Willy exclaimed somewhat sharply.

Listening to the exchange between the two friends, Solita thought with a warm feeling in her heart that Willy, at any rate, was not deceived by the Princess's beauty nor by the seductive way in which she spoke to every man.

She knew instinctively that he disliked the Russians.

She thought it was what she might have expected in someone who had admired her father.

Obediently, because the Duke had told her to do so, she went upstairs to change.

Emily was waiting to help her and was very chatty as she did so.

"Th' Princess was having a fair old 'argy-bargy' with that there brother of hers just now!" Emily was saying.

Solita knew it was wrong, but she could not help asking:

"What about?"

"'Er lady's-maid tells me as 'ow the Prince was findin' fault with her over somethin', and she spat at him like a tiger-cat, and said it wasn't 'er fault!"

"I wonder what could have upset him?" Solita asked vaguely.

"Who knows with 'em foreigners," Emily replied. "Goes off the rails at the slightest thing, they does!"

Solita thought Prince Ivan must have been very annoyed with the Princess for failing to get results with her hypnotism.

"I am sure she will try again," she said beneath her breath.

She prayed that the Duke would make some excuse for not being alone with her.

When she had changed and gone downstairs, it was to find that most of the members of the house-party were assembled in one of the magnificent Salons.

They all seemed to be holding a glass of champagne in their hands.

The Duke had apparently suggested it would be a good start to the expedition.

The Ladies were looking very beautiful.

They were all wearing hats which, even though they were fastened down with large hat pins, looked as if they might blow away at even a breath of wind.

Solita was amused to notice as they moved into the hall that first they covered themselves with what was known as a "dust coat."

Then they put a chiffon scarf over the top of their hats to tie in a bow under their chins.

They did, in fact, look very alluring.

Solita thought her own hat, which was trimmed with small flowers rather than feathers, as was suitable for a young girl, seemed dull by comparison.

She, however, forgot about herself when they set off in the Duke's Phaeton drawn by two magnificently matched chestnuts.

The Countess of Dudley was a great beauty and also very kind.

Although she might have been disappointed at not being alone with the Duke, she was pleasant to Solita.

She pointed out to her, even before the Duke could do so, several of the landmarks which they were passing.

To Solita the countryside itself was a joy with its green meadows, thick woods, and silver streams.

They drove quite a distance on a flat part of the Duke's estate.

Then the two horses started to climb up a hill to where at the top Solita could see the Folly.

It was quite a large one with a high tower, reminiscent of a minaret.

It rose from the strange building which had a Moorish influence in its design.

"My ancestor," the Duke explained, "was an inveterate traveller and brought back many treasures to the Castle. He also built some strange buildings, each one reminding him of his travels."

"This one is certainly unique!" The Countess laughed.

"But very convenient for picnics." The Duke smiled.

'A very luxurious picnic,' Solita thought.

The servants had gone ahead to lay a long table down the centre of the Moroccan building.

Although the food was called "A Cold Collation," there were a dozen different dishes, each more delicious than the last.

There was wine in strangely fashioned goblets which the Duke's ancestor had brought back from Hungary.

The sunshine coming through the unpaned windows seemed to invest everything with a golden glow.

Solita would have found it all very enchanting if she had not been aware that as soon as they arrived the Princess went to the Duke's side.

She then refused to leave him.

"You may sit where you like," the Duke informed his party, "but naturally, the ladies must divide themselves amongst the men."

Before he finished speaking, the Princess had seated herself in a chair beside his at the top of the table.

To her consternation Solita found Prince Ivan beside her.

"Now tell me about yourself, Miss Gresham," he said in a very beguiling voice.

She realised as she looked at him that he was in his own way extremely handsome.

She thought if she had not known so much about him she might have been captivated by the way he talked to her during the meal.

He paid her compliments and was also amusing and witty.

At the same time, she was aware that he was curious as to who she was, and why she was with the Duke.

Solita deliberately made herself sound very young and very girlish.

She told him how she had been brought up in Italy by a Cousin of the Duke's after her parents had died.

She enthused over the youthful parties she had attended, the beauty of Rome, and the music that was so much a part of Italian life.

He appeared to be interested.

Yet she had the uncomfortable feeling that his eyes were looking at her penetratingly.

She thought he was questioning as to whether she was as ingenuous as she appeared.

She therefore talked of how exciting it was to be in England and how the Duke was arranging for his grandmother to present her at a "Drawing Room" at Buckingham Palace.

"It will all be very wonderful," she said, "and I am only afraid that I might make some mistakes."

"I am sure you will never do that!" Prince Ivan said. "And your Guardian will of course protect you from becoming enamoured with the wrong sort of man."

Solita contrived to look surprised.

"I do not think . . . His Grace . . . will worry about me," she said in a shy, girlish voice. "He has . . . so many other things to do."

"And what do you think of him?" the Prince enquired.

"I think he is . . . very kind to worry about anyone as unimportant as me," Solita said with a little giggle, "but, of course, I hope I shall soon make friends of my own age."

She knew as she spoke that the Russian was trying to find out if she was already in love with the Duke.

It was actually something that had never crossed her mind.

She thought that if the Prince asked her the question point-blank, she would truthfully be able to say "No!"

It was only then that a new idea struck her.

If the Duke had done the things the Russians suspected, he was really very different from how she had thought him to be.

She had hated him when she was in Italy, where he paid no attention to her.

He had forgotten her and his Cousin.

When he became a Duke she imagined him attending Receptions and Balls in London every night.

He would, she thought, be present at every Race Meeting, and not giving a thought to those he had known when he was an unimportant soldier.

Now, if he had been engaged in "The Great Game," he was in her estimation a hero.

It was the son of her Aunt Mildred's friends who had told Solita most indiscreetly about "The Great Game."

He was a young Englishman who had travelled a great deal abroad because his father was a Diplomat.

Clive was nineteen, rather conceited, and intended writing a book of his travels.

"It would," he boasted, "astound the world!"

Because Solita was prepared to listen to him talking about himself, which was his favourite subject, he spent quite a lot of time with her.

While his mother and Mildred Leigh were gossiping together about "the good old days" when they were young girls, Clive talked.

It was exciting for Solita, who was always curious about India, to hear about his visit to that country.

He told her about the importance of the Viceroy, the beauty of the Palaces of the Maharajahs, and the strange customs of the Hindus.

"Are you going to put all this in your book?" Solita had asked.

"That, and a great deal more," he said, "but I found out something when I was in India which has never been written about!"

"What is that?" she enquired.

"It is an espionage which the English have invented," he replied.

He lowered his voice as he went on:

"I found out about it quite by accident, and was told never to mention it to a living soul!"

"But please tell me!" Solita begged. "I swear I will not tell anybody."

Because he was a talker, the young man told her of what he had learnt about "The Great Game."

"Think of it," he said excitedly, "there are men all over India, some English, but most of them Indian, fighting secretly against the Russians!"

"It sounds thrilling!" Solita said.

"It is to those who take part in it," was the reply,

"and I wish only that I were one of them!"

"Did you suggest to anyone that you would like to be a member?"

The young man laughed.

"There is not much chance of that!" he said. "If you mention it to any Englishman, he just looks blank and says he does not know what you are talking about."

He bent forward towards Solita as he added in a conspiratorial tone:

"That is why I am going back to India. I am going to find out everything I can about it and put it in my book."

"And I shall read every word of it!" Solita promised loyally.

It intrigued her and it also seemed somehow connected with her father.

She had therefore tried during the next few years to discover from every man she met who had been in India something about "The Great Game."

The elderly Generals who visited Aunt Mildred behaved as she had been told they would, by feigning complete ignorance.

There were only two who were a little more communicative.

"Now tell me why a pretty young girl like you should want to bother her head over what is happening in India!" they said lightly.

Then, perhaps in answer to the pleading in her eyes, they went on:

"Any man who is in 'The Great Game' takes his life in his hands. The participators are the 'unsung heroes.' I know that a friend of mine, who died in a very peculiar manner, was one of them."

There were just little snippets of information.

Yet put together they formed a picture in Solita's mind, and made her more determined than she was already to avenge her father's death.

Now it was obvious that the Duke had played his part in "The Great Game."

It was impossible for her not to reverse completely everything she had thought about him as being "indifferent, selfish, and unkind."

He had been fighting, as her father had fought, for his country.

Also, as her father had done, he had trusted a woman who was treacherous and dangerous.

'I saved him last night,' she thought, 'but what will happen tonight?'

The thought occupied her mind during the afternoon.

When they drove back to the Castle for tea, she longed to talk to the Duke and beg him once again to be careful.

He had, however, made his plans very clear to everybody.

The horses were brought round to the front door before the ladies had sipped their tea or the men had finished their champagne.

Solita had not expected him to go off so soon.

She realised, therefore, that she would not have time to change again into her riding habit.

She was also aware that none of the ladies were riding.

She thought it would look as if she was pushing herself forward and perhaps annoy the Princess if she went off alone with the men.

She therefore watched them wistfully as they rode away.

They were laughing amongst themselves, the Duke

riding an even more magnificent horse than he had ridden that morning.

'Perhaps we can ride again tomorrow,' Solita thought consolingly.

Then, instead of going back to the Drawing Room, she went upstairs to her bedroom.

She was wondering despairingly as she did so what would happen during the night.

Emily helped her out of the gown she had worn at luncheon time into her pretty negligee.

"Now you get into bed, Miss," she said, "an' have a little nap. You was up earlier than any of th' other ladies this mornin' an' you're sure to be late t'night."

"I will do exactly as you say." Solita smiled.

She got into bed and saw beside it the book she had borrowed from the Princess's Boudoir.

Then she had been so bemused by what she had overheard that she had carried it away without thinking.

She turned over the pages, then a sudden idea struck her.

Last night, when she had returned to her own bedroom, she had locked the door of the room she had entered inadvertently.

In case anybody should be aware of what she had done, she had taken away the key and put it into one of the drawers of her dressing table.

Now she was aware that she could, if she wished, unlock the door into the Princess's Boudoir.

She thought it over for a long time, knowing that to enter the room again was taking a great risk.

If she was discovered, and it was quite likely at this time of the day, it might strike the Princess that she had overheard what had been said the night before.

Then she remembered that it was very unlikely the

Princess, or Prince Ivan for that matter, would expect her to be able to speak Russian.

There had been a Russian girl at her school in Italy, who was the daughter of the Russian Ambassador to Rome.

She was a clever girl, the same age as Solita.

At first Solita had avoided her because she hated everybody of the same nationality as those who had killed her father.

Then, and she thought now it was Fate, she had sworn to herself that she would avenge his death, and it might be imperative for her to be able to understand the language of the enemy.

Accordingly, she had deliberately made friends with Olga and helped her with her Italian lessons.

In return, as she was very grateful, the girl was persuaded to teach her Russian.

After two years Olga declared that Solita spoke it as well as she did herself.

Solita looked up at the clock and saw that it was nearly half-past five.

As she did so, she was aware that when the Gentlemen had all gone riding after tea, two of the Duke's guests were not among them.

One was a quite elderly man, a distinguished Statesman, who walked with a limp.

The other was Prince Ivan.

He had been in riding clothes, but at the last moment he appeared to change his mind and the others went without him.

Now it seemed to Solita there was a very good reason for him not joining them.

It was then that she thought he was trying to discover something useful from the elderly Statesman.

She sat up in an agitated way.

It seemed as if the Russians were like a great octopus with their tentacles going out in every direction.

They were dragging first this person, then the other, towards them, and slowly imprisoning them so that there was no escape.

She sat thinking for what seemed a long time, then she decided it was worth the risk.

Even if she were caught she had the book to prove she was only returning it to the shelf.

She got out of bed and picking up the book walked just as she was in her nightgown across the room.

Taking the key from the drawer, she unlocked the door of the Boudoir.

As she turned the handle, there was no sound of anyone speaking.

It was unlikely that the Princess would rest anywhere except in her bed.

Saying a little prayer that she was not mistaken, Solita opened the door.

She was right.

The room was empty except for the fragrance of flowers and the evening sunshine coming through the uncurtained windows.

She went first to the bookcase at the end of the room from where she had taken the volume in her hand.

Then on tiptoe she moved towards the door.

It was closed, and as she stood with her ear against it she heard a door slam.

A second later she heard the Prince's voice.

"It was a damned waste of time," he said, "and I wish to God I had gone riding!"

"I told you he was not of any great importance," the

Princess replied. "We seem to be out of luck at the moment."

"Not at all," the Prince replied. "I have an idea, and I think it is the best I have had for some time."

"What is it?" the Princess asked.

Then as the Prince did not speak she added:

"Lock the door and come and lie down beside me. It is a long time, darling, since we have been alone together."

"I know," the Prince said, "and I have missed you. Curse Calverleigh. I am jealous of him!"

"There is no need for you to be jealous of anyone, as you well know!" the Princess answered in a caressing tone.

There was a sharp click as the Prince turned the key in the lock.

As he did so, Solita very, very softly turned the handle of the communicating door.

It opened without a sound and she left it slightly ajar, as it had been the night before.

Then she heard the Prince making a movement which she was sure meant he was taking off his coat.

He flung himself down on the bed, and a second later she knew he was kissing the Princess.

It seemed to her extraordinary, as they were brother and sister.

But for the moment it was important to listen and not to think.

"Zenka, my darling!" the Prince said passionately.

"Tell me your idea first," the Princess begged, "then we can talk of love."

"It suddenly came to me when we were driving back after luncheon," the Prince said, "what you must do is to marry the Duke!"

"Marry the Duke?" the Princess repeated with a note of surprise in her voice. "But suppose, just suppose—"

"Wait a minute," the Prince said. "I have thought it all out. You marry Calverleigh, and after you have done so you tell him you have discovered that your husband Kozlovski is still alive."

"Do you think he will believe that?" the Princess asked.

"He will have difficulty proving otherwise when there are hundreds, no thousands of Kozlovskis in Russia! To save his face at being married to a bigamist, which of course would cause a scandal, he pays you to disappear."

"How much do you think he will pay?" the Princess asked.

"I should certainly start at one hundred thousand pounds," the Prince said, "and what is more, when you leave for your own country, never to return to England, you take most of the Calverleigh family jewels with you!"

The Princess laughed.

"Oh, Ivan, it is a Fairy Story! Do you really think anyone will believe it?"

"What can he do?" the Prince asked. "Admit his Duchess is a bigamist? Sue you for stealing the family jewels, which would only make the scandal worse than it was already?"

The Princess laughed again.

"You are brilliant, my sweet, absolutely brilliant! No one but you could think of anything so clever!"

"All you have to do," the Prince went on in a serious tone, "is to get him up the aisle. I suggest you get him even more bemused than he is at the moment, then say you want to be married very quietly here in the Chapel."

"I would really like a grand wedding, which would be rather different from the one I had with Alexander, simply because I was carrying his child."

"You will have a quiet wedding!" the Prince said firmly. "The less publicity there is before the ring is on your finger, the better. After that, His Grace the Duke is hooked."

"I see exactly what you mean."

"All you have to do," the Prince went on, "is to get him to propose to you and after that to leave everything in my hands."

"Do I ever want to do anything else?" the Princess asked. "Oh, darling, wonderful Ivan, why do I need to take any other lover when I have you?"

"The answer is quite simple," the Prince said savagely. "We cannot afford to be together as we want to be. We want money, Zenka, and one hundred thousand pounds—no, dammit, two hundred thousand will enable us to spend at least a year or two together in comfort!"

"That is all I want, to be with you," the Princess said caressingly, "and to know that for a short while, at any rate, no other man need touch me!"

There was silence, and Solita knew they were kissing each other.

Very, very softly, as she had done last night, she tiptoed back to her own room.

Solita locked the communicating door, replaced the key in the drawer, then sat down at the dressing table to stare at her reflection with unseeing eyes.

How could she have guessed that there was so much wickedness in the world, or that anyone would think out such a dastardly plot against the Duke?

She realised now that Prince Ivan was not Princess Zenka's brother, but her lover.

He had no money and what they received from General Tcherivin for spying was not enough.

They wanted a large sum of money, and who was more capable of paying it than the Duke?

It was the lowest form of blackmail, and she could understand how he would shrink from the scandal that would ensue if he was proved to have knowingly or unknowingly married a bigamist.

Even worse, an inquiry might reveal that the woman he had married was a spy.

"I have to save him!" Solita said. "But . . . how? How can . . . I do . . . so?"

She had the feeling that the Princess would use every form of Black Magic, as well as hypnotism to get the Duke into her clutches.

She seemed to remember hearing of certain drugs that were used in Russia to force victims to do what was required of them, because their willpower was lost.

It was her young friend Clive who had told her about the tortures that he had learnt about in different parts of Europe.

Those that he had discovered in Russia made Solita put her hands over her ears and refuse to listen to him.

"You are making me feel sick!" she protested.

"It will all be in my book," he said triumphantly, "every word of it, and I shall sell millions of copies, and, like Lord Byron become famous overnight!"

"Lord Byron wrote beautiful poetry," Solita flashed.

"It shocked people when it was published," Clive replied, "and people will be shocked by my book, but they will read it—you wait and see! They will read it!"

Solita rose from the stool in front of the dressing-table to walk about the room.

She knew now that she had to see the Duke alone.

Yet she was desperately afraid that it might be difficult.

She had the idea that the Princess was unaware that their rooms were next to each other.

Because the Duke had spoken so seriously of the danger she was in as well as himself, she thought it would be foolish to reveal it even inadvertently.

Finally she went to the French *secretaire* which stood in a corner of the room and sat down.

She took a sheet of heavily crested writing paper from its leather stand and put it down in front of her.

As she looked at it she knew how frightened she was, frightened of everything.

The octopus was approaching her, its tentacles reaching out to catch her.

Perhaps already the servants were imprisoned by them, and anything she wrote as well as anything she said would be dangerous.

At last she wrote in her pretty, flowing handwriting just a few words:

> *"I must talk to you and although I am sorry to
> be a bore when you are so busy, it is important! I
> did enjoy the picnic today,*
>
> *Love—Solita*

She read carefully what she had written and thought it was the kind of girlish note that was unlikely to make anybody suspicious.

She put it into an envelope and rang the bell.

As she did so she remembered to unlock the outer door, then quickly got into bed.

Emily appeared within a few minutes.

"Did you ring, Miss?" she asked.

"Yes, Emily," Solita replied, "I have here a note for His Grace. Could you get his Valet to put it in his bedroom so that he will see it when he comes upstairs to dress for dinner?"

"Yes, of course, Miss."

Solita lowered her voice.

"Do not," she said, "let the Princess's lady's-maid know about it! I think, although it seems absurd, that she is jealous if His Grace pays attention to anybody else."

"That's true enough," Emily said with a sniff. "We don't want 'er scratching your eyes out, that's for sure!"

"I do not want to upset anyone," Solita said, "but I rarely get a chance to speak to His Grace when we are downstairs."

"The Princess'll take care of that," Emily said. "Leave it t'me, Miss, I'll give it to Mr. Higgins."

"Thank you, Emily, I knew I could rely on you," Solita said.

Emily left, and Solita lay back against her pillows.

There was nothing she could do now but pray she would make the Duke understand.

He was in a different sort of danger from the one he had been in last night, and this was even more frightening.

"Save him...God! Please...save him!" she prayed.

She felt somehow that God was listening to her.

chapter six

SOLITA dressed early, then walked about her room waiting impatiently for a reply to her note.

Finally when she thought despairingly that the Duke had either not received it, or else he had not understood, there was a knock on the door.

Emily went to answer it, and to Solita's relief she heard Higgins, the Duke's Valet, speaking.

Emily came back to her.

"His Grace says," she said slowly, "will you take t' Solicitors letter to 'im in the Study, Miss, at seven-thirty. He'll 'ave time to discuss it with you before dinner."

Emily was obviously repeating laboriously what she had been told to say, but to Solita, it was like the voice of angels.

The Duke understood!

She thought his reply was very clever and would not be of any interest if the servants heard it.

She finished dressing, then, realising that she too must play her part impeccably, searched for a letter in her trunk.

By a strange coincidence it was a letter which had actually come from her Aunt Mildred's Solicitors in Naples.

She ran down the stairs and opened the door of the Study to find the Duke waiting for her.

She shut the door behind her, then said breathlessly:

"You understood! I was so frightened you would think I was just being tiresome."

"Of course I understood," he said in his deep voice, "but tell me quickly what is troubling you."

Breathlessly, because it was so important and she was afraid there was not time to say it all, Solita began:

"I went into the Princess's Boudoir again, just in case there was something more I might find out."

The Duke frowned.

"You should not have taken such a risk," he said sharply.

"I carried with me the book I brought away last night without realising I was doing so."

"At the same time," the Duke said, "the Princess might have discovered you and been suspicious. For Heaven's sake, Solita, this is not a game."

"I know that," Solita replied, "but, please listen."

She told the Duke exactly what she had overheard and saw his expression turn from interest to incredulity, and then anger.

As Solita finished he exclaimed:

"I can hardly believe you are not reading some wildly imaginative drama!"

"You believe me?" Solita asked.

"Of course I believe you," the Duke replied, "but I had no idea that at my age and with my experience I could be so easily deceived!"

There was a bitterness in the way he spoke that made Solita say hastily:

"The Princess is obviously very experienced, and as she is so beautiful, of course men want to believe her."

"It makes me furious!" the Duke said savagely. "And I will never trust any woman again."

"And . . . Prince Ivan is not . . . her brother," Solita said in a low voice a little shyly.

The Duke was silent for a moment, then he said:

"Now you have to help me, Solita, and there is no time to brief you in what I intend to do."

She looked at him apprehensively, and he went on:

"Whatever occurs, we are leaving. Behave naturally, as you would do if there were nothing sinister behind what I do or say."

Solita's eyes widened but she did not interrupt as the Duke said:

"In front of your maid do not say anything she might remember later as being strange."

"I understand."

The Duke smiled at her.

"I know I can rely on you," he said, "and thank you, Solita, for taking a risk which I would never have allowed, had I been aware of it."

He put out his hand towards her as he spoke and taking it Solita said:

"Be careful, for . . . you too . . . must not take any risks."

"I promise you I will be careful," the Duke said. "Now go into the Drawing Room, make yourself pleasant, and talk excitedly about what we are going to do tomorrow."

There were a thousand questions Solita wanted to ask him.

Yet she knew it was imperative that as few people as possible should be aware that they had been alone together.

She therefore hurried back to the hall.

She saw to her relief that there was nobody there to observe where she came from except for the footmen on duty.

She went into the Drawing Room to find that half the house-party were already downstairs talking and drinking champagne.

As she crossed the room Willy came towards her to say:

"You look as though you have had a good rest and are ready to enjoy the festivities which will take place tonight."

"What are they?" Solita asked.

"Our host is being very secretive about it," Willy replied. "But I will tell you one thing you will enjoy, and that is that we are to dance to what I think is one of the best Bands in London."

"How exciting!" Solita exclaimed.

She thought as she spoke that there seemed rather few people for there to be a Ball.

As if Willy followed her thoughts he said:

"There are a number of neighbours coming here after dinner, so you will not be short of partners."

"I hope you are right," Solita said, "because I am fond of dancing."

"I insist that you give me the first dance," Willy said, "otherwise I know I will not get a look in!"

She laughed at him, and they moved towards the fireplace.

The Princess had not yet appeared.

When she did, Solita knew that treacherous and wicked though she was, it would be difficult for any woman to look more beautiful.

She was wearing a crimson gown, very bejewelled, which made her appear as if she were dressed in flames.

Every time she moved, the embroidery on the gown glittered dazzlingly.

So did the huge ruby necklace and a tiara of the same gems which rested on her dark hair.

"Even though I hate her," Solita said to herself, "I have to admit she looks magnificent!"

The Duke arrived a little later full of apologies.

"Forgive me," he said first to the Princess, "but I have some urgent letters to write so that they can be taken to London early tomorrow morning."

"I missed you," the Princess said in a low voice that only he could hear.

Then he was talking to his other guests until unexpectedly he started to sneeze.

He sneezed half-a-dozen times and not only blew his nose, but wiped his eyes as if they were running.

Solita looked at him apprehensively, but he began talking quite animatedly again until dinner was announced.

He offered his arm to the Princess and they led the way while Solita was taken in by Willy.

Just as they reached the Dining Room the Duke had another bout of sneezing.

Solita noticed that the Princess moved a little distance from him as if she were afraid he was contagious.

"I do apologize," the Duke said in a thick voice as he took his seat. "I suppose I must have caught a cold this morning when I went riding before breakfast."

"It sounds to me rather like a recurrence of your old complaint," Willy remarked.

"Nonsense!" the Duke said sharply. "I am sure it is nothing of the sort!"

The food at dinner was delicious, but Solita found it hard to concentrate on anything but the Duke.

The Princess was enticing him with her eyes, her lips, and with every movement of her body.

It was, Solita thought, such a clever performance that she found it hard to believe that she was really in love with Prince Ivan.

The Prince was fortunately at the other end of the table.

He was flirting with the beautiful Lady Dudley, Solita noticed, and it was clear from the expression on her face and the smile in her eyes that she was enjoying herself.

'No one could act more convincingly than they do!' Solita thought.

As course followed course, the Duke did not seem to eat very much, and once or twice he blew his nose.

He was, Solita thought, rather quieter than usual and seemed to be listening to the Princess rather than talking.

Then after dessert had been served and the servants withdrew, he suddenly had another sneezing fit.

This one was certainly worse than the last.

He sneezed and sneezed until it was impossible for anyone at the table to go on talking.

They all stopped and stared at him until he put out his hand as if to find support and rose unsteadily to his feet.

As he did so, Willy jumped up from the table and hurried to his side.

The Duke was still sneezing as he clung to Willy, who put his arm around him.

Then, as if he knew it was what the Duke wanted, he led him towards the Dining Room door.

He had almost reached it when Solita realized the

Duke was actually collapsing, and it was difficult for Willy to hold him up.

She ran to the Duke's other side to support his left arm and they moved out of the Dining Room.

Then, as somebody closed the door behind, Solita could hear the voices of the guests as they all started to chatter at once.

Slowly Willy and Solita escorted the Duke down the passage into the hall.

As they started to climb the stairs the Duke put his arm on Solita's shoulders so that he could use her as a crutch.

It seemed a long way up the stairs and along the corridor which led to the Duke's room.

The Butler, who had followed them, kept asking anxiously if there was anything he could do to help.

Only as Willy opened the door of the Duke's room did he say:

"Fetch Higgins!"

"Very good, Sir," the Butler replied, and hurried away.

As they entered the Duke's bedroom he suddenly stood upright and said:

"Thank you! I thought I gave an impeccable performance!"

"Dammit all!" Willy said. "Do you mean to say I have been wasting my muscles dragging you all this way for a joke?"

The Duke glanced towards the door.

"This is no joke, Willy, and I need your help!"

The way he spoke made an alert look come into Willy's eyes.

"What is happening?"

"Solita has discovered that the Princess is working

for Tcherevin," the Duke replied in a low voice.

Willy stared at him.

"By God! And you had no idea of it?"

"Not until Solita overheard her talking in Russian to Prince Ivan who, incidentally, is her lover and not her brother."

Willy glanced at Solita as if he found it hard to believe that she spoke Russian, but the Duke continued:

"As the Princess is to either hypnotise or drug me into marriage, I have to get away."

"Marriage!" Willy exclaimed.

"Listen," the Duke said, "you have to convince the house-party that I am suffering from a complaint I have had before. Some strange disease I caught when I was in the East."

"What happens then?"

"I will tell you the next step when you come to see me after all the guests who are coming in to dance have left."

"I will do my best," Willy said.

The Duke smiled.

"We have been in tight spots before, Willy, but this is one of the most unpleasant, and I rather suspect, the most dangerous!"

Willy nodded, and Solita realised that if the Duke had been involved in "The Great Game," so had Willy.

"Now, do exactly as I say," the Duke said. "You must both go back to the party and say how worried you are about me, but you are certain I shall be all right by tomorrow."

Solita gave a little cry.

"How can I leave you?" she said. "Supposing the Princess . . . ?"

"I will be all right," the Duke interrupted quietly.

"Higgins will be with me, and I will be guarded."

As he spoke, the door opened and his Valet came in.

He was a thin, wiry man who had obviously been a soldier.

There was something alert about him, which made him different from any ordinary servant.

"It worked, Higgins," the Duke said, "but the pepper you gave me has made my nose raw!"

"It's very effective, Your Grace," Higgins said in a satisfied tone.

"I was just reassuring Miss Gresham and Captain Denham that you will be guarding me tonight so that no one can enter unawares."

"That's right, Your Grace. You can be sure o' that!"

"Higgins is also packing," the Duke said, "my things and yours, Willy."

"And when are we leaving?" Willy asked.

He spoke in a conversational tone, as if there were nothing dramatic or unexpected about what was happening.

"There is a train at six-thirty tomorrow morning."

"You are not leaving me behind?" Solita said in a frightened tone.

"No, of course not," the Duke replied, "but you will have to pack for yourself because nobody in the house must be aware of what we are doing until we have actually left."

Solita felt her heart leap.

All she wanted was to be with the Duke, and not be left behind with the Princess and Prince Ivan.

"Now go back to the party, both of you," the Duke ordered. "You come and see me later, Willy, and, Solita, Higgins will call for you at six o'clock."

"I will be ready," Solita replied.

"For God's sake, take care of yourself," Willy said to the Duke.

Now there was a note in his voice that told Solita he was aware of how dangerous the Russians could be.

"Leave everythin' t' me, Captain," Higgins said. "I'll see 'Is Grace comes to no harm from the 'Ruskies.' There's not one o' them I'd trust further than I could throw 'em!"

"You are right there!" Willy smiled.

As he spoke he put out his hand to Solita, and taking hers he said:

"Come on, we have to face the music and make no mistakes."

They walked towards the door together, but she looked back at the Duke.

"I shall be 'praying,'" she said softly, "that you will be all right."

"Your prayers are very important," the Duke replied unexpectedly.

Willy pulled her through the door and shut it behind him.

"Sometime," he said in a low voice, "I want you to explain to me a great many things, including how you can speak Russian."

Solita smiled because he was obviously so surprised, and he went on:

"We are worried about the Duke, but feel he will be all right by morning."

"I understand."

"They are like vipers, and as poisonous as cobras!" Willy said bitterly.

* * *

Downstairs, the Ladies had moved into the Drawing Room while the Gentlemen were still enjoying their port.

As Solita joined the former, the Princess asked:

"What is happening? Where is our dear and generous host?"

"I am afraid he is not very well," Solita said in a little-girl voice, "but his Valet is with him, and I think he will be quite all right in the morning."

"That is good news!" several Ladies murmured.

Solita, however, was aware that the Princess was annoyed, although she did not say anything.

When the Gentlemen joined them, she called Willy to her side.

"What are you doing about Hugo?" she enquired. "Surely you should send for the doctor?"

"I think he will be all right," Willy replied blithely. "The local 'Sawbones' would have no idea how to treat these very unpleasant attacks, which are a recurrence of some fever he caught in Malaya or some such outlandish place!"

"Will he have it for long?" the Princess asked.

Solita knew, although it seemed quite an obvious question, that it was to the Princess a vital one.

"Good heavens, no!" she replied. "Hugo has the strength of a horse, and once these sneezing fits are over he will be himself again."

"That makes me very happy." The Princess smiled benignly.

Willy leant towards her and said:

"But he will not be able to join us tonight, and I know he would want you to act as hostess."

Solita saw a light come into the Princess's eyes, and knew that nothing could have pleased her more.

She was only too willing to establish her position at the Castle.

As the other guests arrived she greeted them, directing everybody into the Ballroom, where the Band was already playing.

She started off the dancing herself with the most distinguished guest present.

Solita danced with Willy.

She knew it would be a great mistake to talk of anything that might be overheard, or worse still, the Russians might be capable of lip-reading.

She had heard so many things about them.

She knew she dare not risk making them suspicious by even, as the Duke had said, the flicker of an eyelid.

She tried to make everyone aware that she was excited at being able to dance and how much she was enjoying herself.

She felt a little wistfully that she would really have been enjoying it a great deal more if the Duke had been present, also, if there were not a dark shadow hanging over their heads.

It was one o'clock before the guests who had come to the Castle from neighbouring houses began to leave.

It was a quarter-to-two before Solita could go up to bed, as it was then that the Countess of Dudley and the other Ladies who were staying in the house retired.

As she reached the top of the stairs she heard the Princess behind her say to Willy:

"I must just go and say goodnight to our dear Duke. I would not wish him to feel he was being neglected."

"I feel sure none of us will be allowed to do that," Willy replied.

"Why not?" the Princess enquired.

"Because when Hugo is ill his Valet, who has been

with him for years, is more belligerent than a bulldog."

He smiled as he went on:

"In fact, that is a rather good description. I know that Higgins will watch over him all night, in case he has another attack."

"Do you mean he will be in the same room?" the Princess asked curiously.

"I expect so, or else in the dressing-room, with the door open," Willy replied. "Higgins is like an old Nanny who enjoys it when the children are at their mercy!"

He laughed as if he had made a joke, but Solita was sure that the Princess was looking angry.

She delayed going to her room until she had seen the Princess go into hers and shut the door.

Then she went into her bedroom and started to pack.

* * *

Solita found it was impossible to sleep.

She had finished packing her trunk which, being small, had fortunately been left in a cupboard opening off her room.

She pulled back the curtain and lay down on her bed, waiting for the first light of dawn.

When it came she dressed herself in the pretty travelling gown in which she had arrived at the Castle.

She put over it a long cape which she had found extremely useful in keeping out the cold when she had crossed the Channel.

She could hardly dare to hope that, as the Duke had said, they were going to India.

But she had to be prepared for anything.

At five minutes to six there was a very gentle tap on her door, and Higgins looked in.

"You're ready, Miss?" Higgins asked in a whisper.

Solita nodded, knowing it would be a mistake to talk more than was necessary.

Higgins picked up her trunk and carried it out of the room, and Solita followed him.

As she reached the staircase she saw at the bottom of it the Duke, wrapped in blankets, being carried down the stairs by two footmen, with Willy supervising them.

They moved out through the front door and down the long flight of stone steps.

There was a closed carriage waiting for them.

The Duke was placed carefully on the back seat, and Solita and Willy occupied the narrow one facing it.

Solita had seen there was a Brake behind the carriage which contained their luggage, so she knew Higgins would follow them to the station.

"Look after everything, Dawson," Willy said to the Butler. "You know His Grace relies on you."

"I'll do my best, Sir," the Butler replied, "and I'll pray that His Grace is not as bad as he looks!"

"He will be all right once we get him to a doctor who knows how to treat this particular complaint," Willy replied.

They drove off and Solita, looking at the Duke, was suddenly aware that he did look very ill.

His face was very pale, his eyes were closed, and shrouded in blankets he appeared to be a real invalid.

Then as they passed down the drive the Duke opened his eyes.

"I am suffocating in these infernal blankets!" he said. "Can I take them off now?"

"Not until we are on the train," Willy said. "You know how servants talk. Your servants must relay to everybody at the Castle how ill you looked."

The way he spoke was so funny that the Duke gave a little chuckle.

"I wonder how you would like being trussed up like an old hen?" he asked.

"You know I loathe discomfort," Willy said, "as I told you when we were perishing with cold on that mountain with two dozen ferocious tribesmen wanting to take pot-shots at us!"

"This time the enemy is female," the Duke replied.

Solita bent towards him.

"You must tell me what you have planned," she said. "I have been worrying all night in case the Princess was suspicious."

"She certainly would be suspicious," the Duke replied, "if she had any idea where we were going. That is why we have to be very, very careful!"

Now he spoke in a serious tone which made Solita aware that they were still in danger.

As if Willy were thinking the same thing, he said:

"Let us talk about it on the train. It is safer there. Shut your eyes, Hugo, and look half-dead!"

"That is what I feel in this heat," the Duke replied.

He did not speak again until they reached the station.

There were two of the Duke's senior servants to supervise getting him on the platform and into his private coach.

He was placed very gently on a large sofa.

A few minutes later a Goods Train arrived to which the coach was attached.

The Duke's servants arranged everything, and it was only a little more than ten minutes before the train moved off.

They were on their way to London.

It was then, when the Halt was out of sight, that the

Duke threw off his blankets. Solita saw that underneath them he was dressed in his everyday clothes, except for his coat.

"That was a good performance!" Willy said. "And I commend you, Hugo, on not having lost your skill!"

"Keep your fingers crossed!" the Duke replied. "We are not 'out of the wood' yet by any means!"

As he spoke Higgins came in from the Pantry with their breakfast.

Solita realised that it had been brought aboard the train in hay-baskets to keep it as hot as was the coffee which they all drank thirstily.

When Higgins had left, Willy said:

"Come on, Hugo, tell us what plans you have made."

The Duke had finished his eggs and bacon, and Solita thought the food was excellent.

He was now spreading a pat of thick golden Jersey butter on a piece of freshly-baked bread.

He added some honeycomb before he replied:

"I have been up most of the night writing letters; the first, of course, to Kimberley."

"Did you tell him what you had discovered?" Willy asked.

"I told him everything, and that it was extremely important that the Russians should have no idea that we were going to India."

"Do you think he will be able to keep it quiet?" Willy asked.

"The servants at the house will be told that on doctor's orders I have to go to a Spa in France which treats Oriental diseases."

"I hope the Russians believe that!" Willy said a little doubtfully. "What did you tell the Princess?"

"I wrote her a very affectionate letter begging her to help me by acting as hostess to the house-party and keeping them amused. I also told her there was no reason for her or her brother to leave until later in the week."

"Do you think she will stay as long as that?"

"I think," the Duke said slowly, "she will be quite busy planning what alterations she will make to the Castle when she is my wife!"

Solita gave a stifled little cry of protest and he said:

"It is all right. You warned me, and by the time we return to England, I think the Princess will have left the country for good!"

"Why should she do that?" Willy asked curiously.

"I told Kimberley what Solita had discovered, that Prince Ivan is not her brother, but her lover."

"What do you think he will do with that information?" Willy asked.

"Kimberley is very clever at that sort of thing," the Duke said complacently. "He will drop just a suspicion into the ears of the best-known gossips. You know how easy it is. . . ."

The Duke spoke in a slightly affected voice as he said:

"I was told the other day, but of course it is absolute nonsense, that the beautiful Princess Zenka, whom they had known since she was a young girl, never had a brother! Naturally, it is a ridiculous idea!"

Willy laughed.

"No one could resist repeating that!"

"It will be repeated and repeated," the Duke said with satisfaction, "until you know as well as I do that the doors of Mayfair will all close, one after another.

Women always suspect that women who are too beautiful cannot be trusted!"

Willy laughed again, and Solita thought it was very clever of the Duke.

She had heard the gossip that took place in France and Italy amongst the important hostesses.

They would never tolerate anyone whose reputation was in the least questionable.

She knew the Duke was right, and any rumour would spread like wildfire.

Whether or not anybody troubled to verify the story, the Princess would be ostracised.

"What do you want me to do?" Willy asked as if he had just thought of it.

"I want you to come with Solita and me to India!"

Willy looked at him in surprise.

"You really want me?"

"I want a chaperon," the Duke said. "I am Solita's Guardian. At the same time, she is far too pretty to travel around the world with a man unless he was old enough to be her grandfather!"

"You are getting on that way," Willy joked, "but I suppose I must sacrifice myself to help you!"

"I need you," the Duke said quietly, "in case things get rough!"

Solita clasped her hands together.

She knew without him elaborating the point that they were in grave danger.

If the Russians suspected for one moment what they were doing, they would undoubtedly try to destroy them all before they reached Calcutta.

"I suppose you warned Kimberley not to send anything about us by cable?"

"Of course I did," the Duke said sharply, "even though I was sure it is unnecessary."

He paused, then went on as if he were thinking it out:

"We will arrive as ordinary tourists. The Viceroy is a distant relative of mine, and if we appear unexpectedly he will be quite pleased to see us."

"I hope so," Willy said a little doubtfully. "I would not relish a number of Russian spies waiting to kill us as we step ashore!"

"You are not to frighten Solita!" the Duke admonished him.

She smiled at him because she thought it was so kind of him to think of her.

At the same time, she knew they would be travelling for a long time.

Any of the spies might become aware that the Duke was not having treatment in France as he was supposed to be doing.

"Please God . . . do not let . . . them find out," she prayed.

* * *

When they reached London, and it did not take long, the Duke was carried from the train by his servants, who were waiting on the platform.

Solita learnt that a messenger had been sent from the Castle to London on an earlier train to inform the Duke's secretary that His Grace would be arriving. He also carried a letter of instructions.

Solita was therefore not surprised when almost as soon as they had arrived at Calverleigh House, they were off again.

They drove to Victoria Station to take the train to Dover.

125

She just had time to collect what trunks she wished to take with her.

Some of those she had brought with her from Italy were filled with books, and these she left behind.

There was no time to sort out the others, and they were placed as they were with the Duke's luggage and left with Higgins to attend to.

The Duke's clothes had been packed before they arrived.

Willy went to collect his belongings from his flat in Half Moon Street.

It was, Solita thought, an excellent example of the Duke's genius for organisation that they were able to catch a morning train to Dover.

They were actually moving into the Channel in the Duke's private yacht by luncheon time.

Because he had to continue acting his part as an invalid, the Duke had luncheon in his own cabin.

Solita and Willy ate in the Saloon.

"I can hardly believe this is happening!" she said when they were alone.

"I always feel like that when I am working with Hugo," Willy replied.

"Have you done this sort of thing before often?" Solita enquired.

She was a little shy of asking questions.

She knew that if, as she suspected, the Duke had been involved in "The Great Game," he would never speak of it.

Willy smiled at her.

"When you get to know your Guardian better," he said, "you will realise he is the most fantastic person. He has two personalities—the one he shows to the world, and the one which is known only to his closest friends, like myself."

"I never suspected . . . I never imagined for . . . one moment," Solita said, "that he was . . . anything but an . . . ordinary Englishman."

Willy smiled again.

"That is exactly what he would want people to think. What interests me, however, is how you can have been so intelligent as to have saved him, as he says you have done."

"It was simply because I know Russian."

She paused for a moment before she continued:

"I suppose it is Fate, or perhaps Papa, guiding me, which made me realise when I was at School with girls of so many different nationalities, that although I loathed and detested the Russians, it might be useful to know their language."

"It has certainly proved very useful where Hugo is concerned!" Willy remarked.

"He has told you what the Princess intended?"

"To marry him?" Willy asked in a hard voice. "I am eternally grateful to you, Solita, for saving him from that!"

"I think something much greater than myself, perhaps the Power which Mama believed in, was guiding me."

"I am sure of that," Willy said quietly.

Only when they were leaving Calais aboard the train which was to carry them to Marseilles did the Duke feel he could relax.

He discarded his blankets and washed the powder from his face which had made him look so white.

"Unless they are clairvoyant, I should be able to relax," he said.

Solita gave a little cry.

"But that is exactly what they are!" she said. "So do, please, take care!"

The Duke looked at his watch.

"By this time," he said complacently, "the Princess will be decking herself out to go down to dinner and eclipse every other woman who is at the Castle!"

"You do not think that she and the Prince will have left?" Willy asked.

The Duke smiled.

"I cannot believe any woman could resist staying for as long as possible in the position as Chatelaine and hostess."

Willy laughed.

"I expect you are right."

"It will be a rehearsal for the time when she believes she will reign there as my wife!"

As he spoke he saw a strained expression on Solita's face and asked:

"What is wrong? I have a feeling you dislike me speaking like that."

"I remember someone once saying, I think when I was in Italy," Solita replied, "that the real art of deception was to think one's self into the part."

The Duke looked at her in surprise as she went on:

"The man said: 'If I wish to pretend to be the Prime Minister, I would say to myself over and over again:

"'I am the Prime Minister, I am the Prime Minister! And those who were sensitive to my thoughts would say:

"'I am sure that is the Prime Minister over there!'"

The Duke looked at her.

"What you are really doing, Solita, is rebuking me

for thinking of the Princess, which may make her think of me."

"Yes . . . that was in . . . my mind."

"And you are right," he said. "Of course you are right! Willy, take a lesson from my newest and certainly most intelligent recruit!"

"She is not only right," Willy said, "but she is also very remarkable, and I am very proud to know her."

He spoke so sincerely that Solita blushed.

Then, as she realised that the Duke's eyes were on her, she blushed again and said:

"I want to talk about India. Please, tell me some of your experiences of the country that to me has always been 'El Dorado.'"

"I doubt if you will feel that once you get there," Willy teased. "It is terribly hot. The food and the water will upset you, and you will be harrowed by the poverty of its inhabitants!"

"You will also be enthralled by the beauty of everything," the Duke interposed, "not only the Palaces, the Princes, and the saris, but everywhere you look there are children with huge eyes whose slim, coffee-coloured bodies are entrancing."

Solita clasped her hands together.

"That is what I want you to tell me."

"And what you will soon see for yourself," the Duke remarked.

At Marseilles they boarded a P & O Liner which was on its way to India.

The Duke's secretary, who was the only person to know the truth of where they were going, had engaged four of the best State Cabins.

They were booked in the name of "Lord Durham" which was one of the Duke's minor titles.

It was one, Solita learned, which he usually used when he was travelling, and had a passport made out in that name.

They were welcomed aboard with the respect accorded to a member of the British nobility.

Only when Higgins was unpacking for them did Solita understand why four State Rooms had been booked.

There were no Suites in the ships except for the luxury liners which crossed the Atlantic.

Because the Duke was prepared to pay, one of the State bedrooms was quickly changed into a Sitting Room, where they could be alone and also have their meals.

"I do not want the other people aboard to be too curious about us," the Duke explained, "so the fewer questions we are asked the better."

The way he spoke made Solita aware that it would be disastrous if when they arrived in Calcutta the Russian spies were aware of it.

It would prevent the Duke from finding out how the messages from England were intercepted on the Submarine Cable.

They learnt the ship had had a rough passage in the Bay of Biscay after it had left England.

While Solita believed herself to be a good sailor, she had no wish to put it to the test.

She knew also that by going overland they had shortened the time it would take them to reach Calcutta.

The P & O Liners, now that the Suez Canal was opened, took between seventeen and twenty days to reach India.

Allowing for the three days that must have been lost in coming through the Bay of Biscay, she reckoned they would be in Calcutta in perhaps sixteen days' time.

When she went to bed at night she prayed that nothing would delay them, and for their safety.

It was a very strange voyage in some ways.

Willy and the Duke would exercise themselves by walking around the top deck very late at night or very early in the morning.

Because the Duke thought Solita would create curiosity amongst the older passengers, she would go on the top deck in the morning.

She would do so again in the afternoon, when most of the ladies aboard were having English tea in the Saloon.

The rest of the time she was able to listen to the Duke and Willy being interesting, amusing, and witty.

Just sometimes she was alone with the Duke.

They had passed through the Suez Canal and were reaching the end of the Red Sea when Willy said after dinner one evening:

"I am going to have a game of cards. There is a man aboard who is an acknowledged expert at Bridge; in fact, he is one of the best players in the world and I want to pit my wits against him."

"You will lose your money!" the Duke remarked warningly.

"One always has to pay for experience," Willy quipped.

He went from the cabin, and the Duke, sitting comfortably in an armchair, asked Solita:

"What do you want to do?"

"Talk to you."

"I am afraid this is all rather dull for you," he said. "You really ought to be dancing with the young soldiers who are on board or playing Deck Tennis with them."

"I have a feeling," Solita replied, "that because so

much has happened I am very much older than they are!"

The Duke laughed. Then he said:

"Of course you are right. It is not the years that count. It is what you think and feel that makes you older."

"I am sure that being frightened has done that," Solita said lightly, "in fact, I am surprised that my hair has not turned grey!"

"I am sorry," the Duke said. "This should not be happening to anyone as young and lovely as you."

"I do not think it should happen to anyone, whatever their age!" Solita replied, thinking of the Princess.

The Duke must have read her thoughts, for after a moment he said:

"You are right, but remember—for every dangerous and frightening Russian, there are millions of nice, friendly, ordinary people who would not frighten a mouse!"

"Then I hope I meet them!" Solita answered.

"I promise you," the Duke said, "that when this is over I am taking you back to England where my grandmother will chaperon you and you will be a great social success."

As he spoke Solita suddenly realised it was something she did not want.

She did not want to be a social success. She did not wish to be with his grandmother, but with the Duke.

Even though she admired him, even though she knew in the last few days how different he was from anything she had imagined, she had not understood.

Now she knew why she was so afraid for him.

Every night when she went to bed she prayed with her mind, her heart, and her soul that he would be safe, that nothing terrible would happen to him, now or ever.

It had never crossed her mind, however, that what she felt was love.

Yet now she knew in a blinding flash that he was everything she wanted in a man.

It was not just his cleverness, it was not only his handsome looks.

It was something far deeper, something which made her vibrate to his thoughts, his feelings, and to everything that was him.

"Of course! I love him!" she told herself. "And the only extraordinary thing is that I did not realise it sooner!"

But it was not what she had expected love to be like.

What she felt was he was not only a protection, but a guide, a star twinkling in the sky which she must follow.

'I love him . . . I love him!' she thought.

Then she was aware that the Duke's eyes were on her face.

"What are you thinking?" he asked.

"Of you!" she answered truthfully.

"And what conclusions have you come to?"

"That you are . . . very clever."

"Thank you!" the Duke said mockingly. "But I think you are being kind, seeing how extremely stupid I have been."

"Not stupid," Solita corrected him. "Few men are big enough to admit that they have made a mistake."

"It is one I am quite prepared to admit," the Duke said, "and I could kick myself for being such a fool!"

"There is no need to do that," Solita said. "We all make mistakes, but it is something one should never do twice."

"I will make certain of that!" the Duke said savagely.

Solita rose and walked to the window.

They were on the main deck, and their State Room looked out onto a now empty deck.

The stars were gleaming like diamonds overhead.

She wanted to go outside and look at them, and not be restricted by being in the cabin.

Impulsively, she looked at the Duke.

"Let us go outside," she pleaded.

"It is something I am longing to do," he answered. "I find it stifling in here."

They went out on deck knowing that most of the passengers were in the large Saloon talking.

They would be gambling on the amount of nautical miles the ship had done during the day, while a number of the men, like Willy, were in the Card Room.

The deck was therefore empty, and Solita went to the guard rail to stare out at the sea.

The brilliance of the stars made the great arc of the sky above them fill the whole world.

She raised her head to look up at them unaware that the Duke had come a little nearer to her.

"It is so unbelievably beautiful!" she said in a soft voice.

"And so are you!" he replied.

For a moment she thought she could not have heard him correctly.

Then his arms went round her and he pulled her very gently against him.

For a moment he looked down at her and her eyes seemed to be caught in the starlight.

She was staring at him in surprise and the softness of her mouth trembled because he was touching her.

Then his lips came down on hers.

As he kissed her, Solita knew that this was what her whole body had been longing for.

When she had prayed for him, when she had known just now she loved him, she was giving him herself.

The Duke kissed her at first very gently.

Then, as if the sweetness and innocence of her lips excited him, his kiss became more demanding, more insistent.

To Solita it was as if the stars themselves had come down from the sky, not only to blind her eyes, but were in her heart and in every breath she drew.

She could feel their radiance vibrating from the Duke's mouth to hers.

She thought that if she died at this moment, she would know she had felt ecstacy and touched the perfection of God.

As the Duke raised his head she made a little murmur and turned her face to hide it against his neck.

He held her very close, then with his lips against her forehead he said:

"How have you done this to me, Solita?!"

"D-done . . . what?" she asked.

"Made me feel different that I have ever felt in my whole life before. I did not know that love was like this!"

She looked up at him and said:

"That is what I have been thinking . . . but then I have never known . . . any love."

"Nor have I," the Duke said seriously, "and what I felt in the past has not been love, but I always knew if I could find it, love would be like you and the stars."

Solita made a sound—like a gasp of joy.

"That is what I thought just now when you kissed me, that the stars were on your lips and in my heart."

"As you are in mine," the Duke said.

Then as if he felt he could express himself better by kissing her than words, he kissed her possessively, demandingly, until they were both breathless.

"I love you!" Solita whispered.

As the Duke's arms tightened about her he said:

"And I love you, my darling, but for the moment there is nothing I can do about it."

Solita looked puzzled, and he said:

"When the Princess knows I am in India, I am a marked man, and she will do everything in her power to destroy me."

Solita gave a cry of horror.

"It is true," the Duke said, "and I would not insult your intelligence by pretending otherwise."

"But . . . suppose they . . . kill you?" Solita whispered frantically.

"That is what they will try to do, and that is why, my precious, I have to protect you."

"All I want is to be with you."

"As I want to be with you," the Duke replied. "At the same time, I think now, if I am sensible, when we reach Calcutta, you should remain in the ship."

"No . . . of course not," Solita said quickly. "Do you think I would leave . . . you? Do you think I would . . . trust even Willy to look . . . after you?"

She thought he was going to oppose her, and she said:

"I have . . . saved you . . . twice, and as I believe that . . . everything goes in . . . threes, after the . . . third time you will be . . . a free man!"

The Duke did not answer, he merely moved his lips over her cheek.

She knew he was thinking that because the Princess

was a woman she would consider she had been scorned and would be determined to have her revenge.

Solita moved even nearer to the Duke than she was already.

"We must not be . . . afraid," she whispered. "With God . . . and perhaps a little help from Papa, I have . . . saved you . . . and why should we be . . . afraid now."

The Duke took a deep breath.

"You are right, my darling one," he said, "and I have been blessed as few other men have, and most of all by finding you. We must put our trust in our Karma, as the Indians do, and believe that the gods are on our side, and will not fail us."

"I think," Solita said very softly, "that the gods have given you courage to fight for what you believe is right, and they will not only protect us but fight with us."

"Only you could say something like that."

Then the Duke was kissing her again; kissing her now passionately, fiercely, as if he defied the world to separate them.

Solita felt that her love for him carried her up to the stars.

The light from them was dazzling.

It was a light that would illuminate the darkness and drive away the evil that lurked in it.

chapter seven

By the time they reached Calcutta, Solita was more and more in love.

She was also day by day becoming more and more frightened.

She lay awake at night thinking that the Princess would never forgive the Duke if she knew he had gone to India instead of being in France.

Also, if she had the least suspicion that he was in love with somebody else, she would do everything to avenge herself.

"What can I do?" Solita asked over and over again in the darkness of her cabin.

Even her prayers seemed to receive no answer.

Finally, because she felt the Duke was not taking the situation as seriously as he should, she asked Higgins to bring her up one of her trunks.

In it she had packed when she left Italy all the little souvenirs she had left of her mother's.

Among them there was a small revolver which her mother had carried in India when her father was away.

Because she was so often in the North, where things were more dangerous than in the South, her father had insisted on her mother learning to shoot.

138

He had then given her the smallest and lightest revolver available.

He insisted that if she was alone in the house with only the native servants, she was to carry it with her both by day and by night.

Solita found it wrapped in a carved Indian box which also contained a number of letters from her father to her mother.

There were also little things she treasured, like the programme of the Ball at which they had first met and the poems he had written to her before they were married.

There were a number of bullets to go with the revolver.

She hid it away in her luggage and said nothing about it to the Duke.

She had no idea that he was even more worried than she was.

He, too, would lie awake at night wondering how he could extract himself from the appalling situation he was in.

He knew even better than Solita that the Russian Secret Police had long memories.

If the Princess or Prince Ivan reported that he was working with the Earl of Kimberley or they were suspicious of his activities, he would die.

It could be from a knife thrust by an unknown assailant, poison inserted into his food, or an unaccountable accident which would prove fatal.

"What could I do?" he asked the gods.

Like Solita, he found no answer.

It was some consolation to have Willy with him, who had been with him in so many tight spots before.

Once Willy realised that the Duke and Solita were in love, he was extremely tactful.

He would make every excuse to leave them alone.

He liked playing Deck Quoits with some of the passengers, and spent almost every evening at the Bridge tables.

It was then the Duke would hold Solita in his arms.

As he did so he would wonder despairingly how long they would be together.

The Russian spy must be somewhere at Viceregal Lodge.

The Duke knew the one thing he must not do in any circumstances was to let the man or woman be aware of what he felt for Solita.

The Russians had their own way of communicating with each other, wherever they might be in any part of the world.

There was every chance that the Princess would be advised of his feelings.

Then, as he put it to himself "all hell would break loose."

When the ship stopped at Bombay, a few passengers got off and it then went on to Calcutta.

As they steamed into the harbour the Duke reminded Solita and Willy that he was travelling as "Lord Durham."

"Only the Viceroy will be aware of my correct identity," he said, "but no one else."

"You will be very careful," Solita said. "You know I will be ... praying that your ... mission will be ... successful."

"*Our* mission," the Duke corrected her, "and I am relying on your instinct, my darling, as much as my own."

They looked into each other's eyes.

Willy was aware that they had forgotten for the moment that he even existed.

When they went ashore Solita was wearing one of her prettiest gowns and a very attractive broad-brimmed hat trimmed with flowers.

She carried a sunshade to protect her from the sun, which even though it was early morning, seemed to burn down on them like an open furnace.

Just before they docked, the Captain, on the Duke's instructions, had sent a message to tell the Viceroy of his arrival.

When they stepped ashore there was an open carriage bearing the insignia of the Viceroy waiting for them.

The servants were wearing the Viceregal uniforms with red turbans.

There were also four soldiers on horseback to escort them to the Viceregal Lodge.

Solita had already heard about the splendour of it and that it was the finest Governor's Palace in the world, a symbol of the great British power.

She was, however, not prepared for the overwhelming beauty of its Ionic Pillars, the enormous flight of steps, and the magnificence she was to see later in the great rooms.

The Palace had been built on a site ideally situated to the climate, as it caught the breeze at all four corners.

As they drove up with a flourish to the portico, Solita was thinking only of the Duke.

She loved him and was very frightened of what would occur during the next day or so.

The Duke appeared very much at his ease.

As they walked through the high-ceilinged and exquisitely decorated corridors, there was nothing in his bearing to show that he was even apprehensive.

The Viceroy, Lord Ripon, was waiting for him.

Solita's first impression was that he was a short man with a large beard, decidedly plain with a bulbous nose and a rather donnish expression in his eyes.

Then when he welcomed her, instinct told her that he was a clever man beneath his air of simplicity.

He did not say much to the Duke because not only was Solita there but there was also an *Aide-de-Camp*.

It was only when the Duke was alone in his bedroom that one of the Senior Officials on the Viceroy's staff came to ask him what he wished to do.

"I am very interested to see the workings of the Submarine Cable," he answered, "and Lord Kimberley has asked me to report personally as to whether the messages from the India Office are received quickly and without interference."

There was no need to say more.

The expression on the Official's face told the Duke he understood what he meant. He merely bowed and said:

"Would it be convenient for you, My Lord, to visit the room in which the messages are received after luncheon?"

"Thank you," the Duke replied, "and I would also like to take with me my Ward, and Captain Denham."

"That will be arranged, My Lord," the Official said politely, and left the room.

Alone again, the Duke walked to the window to look out onto the busy compound.

There were numerous people moving about on it, rickshaws travelling from one building to another.

A number of Indians and Europeans who were walking slowly were apparently nothing more than sight-seers.

It seemed to the Duke extraordinary that while everything looked peaceful and quiet, the Russians were ready to destroy the serenity of it.

He, however, went down to luncheon smiling, and as if he were concerned only with enjoying himself.

Like several other Viceroys, Lord Ripon had a very rich wife who had increased his own wealth, which was considerable.

He therefore lived as a *Grandee* even though politically he was very much a Radical.

His appointment had made history, as he was the first Catholic to become a High Officer of State since the seventeenth century.

There were a number of guests at luncheon in the large Dining Room looking onto the beautiful gardens filled with flowers.

The *Punkahs* were working, and the room, with its long, open windows, was cool despite the blazing sun outside.

There were footmen behind every chair, and their white and red uniforms were a supplement to the brilliant colours of the guests' clothes.

Solita felt the whole setting was very picturesque.

But while they talked, laughed, and ate, she felt as if there was a heavy stone within her breast.

Every time she looked at the Duke she found herself praying that this would not be the last time they would enjoy the company of other people.

"How can we . . . live like . . . this?" she asked herself.

As she met the Duke's eyes she knew that despite his relaxed attitude, he was thinking as she was.

Last night, when they had been alone in their State Room on board ship he had held her close in his arms.

"I love you, my precious one," he had said, "and I cannot imagine my life without you."

She looked at him questioningly, and it flashed through her mind that perhaps he was going to send her away from him.

Then he said violently:

"I want you as my wife, I want you close to me by day and by night, but God knows, it is a risk I dare not take!"

"I am not afraid," Solita said, "and if I could be your wife . . . even for a . . . short while . . . it would be the most . . . perfect and . . . wonderful thing that could . . . happen to me."

"And do you think I could bear it, knowing that because you were my wife, the Russians would be as determined to kill you as they are to kill me?" the Duke asked.

"Which they . . . must not . . . do!" Solita cried. "It is wrong . . . wicked, and . . . unfair that you . . . should die in . . . such a way!"

She would have said a great deal more, but the Duke had kissed her.

Then it was impossible to think of anything but the rapture his kisses gave her.

Once again the light of the stars was radiating from them both, and everything that was evil was forgotten.

When luncheon was finished the guests began to take their leave of the Viceroy.

The Official who had visited the Duke in the morning then came to his side.

"If you will come with me, Your Grace, I will take you to the Cipher Office."

Solita drew in her breath.

When she had left the ship she had slipped her mother's revolver into the pocket of her full skirt.

It was intended for a handkerchief and little else, but the pistol was well concealed.

As Solita felt it hard against her hip, it gave her some comfort to know it was there.

She was well aware that the Duke carried no weapon with him.

The previous evening when they were going to bed Willy had asked:

"Do you intend to arm yourself tomorrow when we visit the Cipher Room?"

"Good heavens, no!" the Duke replied. "The Russian spy, if there is one there, could hardly attack me in front of half-a-dozen other people!"

"How do you hope to identify him?" Willy had enquired.

The Duke made a gesture with his hands.

"I have no idea, we must just 'play it by ear.'"

"Do you think he will look like a Russian?" Solita asked.

"There are hundreds of different castes in India," the Duke replied, "all with individual characteristics. They could easily find a traitor in any part of the country."

"How shall we ever know? How shall we ever recognise the man we are seeking?" Willy asked with a despairing note in his voice.

"Solita will say it is by using our instincts," the Duke replied.

"That is what we have to do," Solita said, "and perhaps our vibrations will tell us he is not what he appears to be."

"If you are talking about being clairvoyant, you can

count me out," Willy said sharply. "I have never been any good at that sort of hanky-panky. If a man attacks you, I will knock him down, but it would be easier if you would allow me to take my revolver with me."

"And have an obvious bulge in your coat?" the Duke asked scathingly. "Certainly not!"

Solita said nothing.

But when she got into the carriage to sit beside the Duke, she had been careful to sit so that he was not aware that there was something hard and lumpy in her pocket.

As they walked across the compound to the main building she felt her revolver and thought reassuringly that it was there.

She had not learnt to shoot when she was in Italy with Aunt Mildred.

She would have been horrified at the idea of her doing anything so "unladylike."

It was one of her Italian friends with whom she stayed almost every year who had what they called a "Shooting School" in the basement of their Palazzo.

It was used mainly by her three brothers, who vied with each other in hitting the bull's-eye in the target.

They had been amused when the girls had challenged them.

As Solita and her friend were so eager to do so, the older brother gave them lessons.

"You never know when you might need it," he said, "you could be captured and held for ransom, and it is a good idea for women to know how to shoot as well as men."

It was something Solita wanted to do, so she begged him to give her a lesson almost every day when she was staying in Rome.

By the time she was seventeen and so lovely that he was paying her extravagant compliments, he was only too willing to do anything she asked.

When she finally hit the bull's-eye three times in succession from quite a long distance, he tried to kiss her.

She had resisted him and continued with her shooting lessons by making quite sure they were never alone.

Now she thought how wise she had been.

Perhaps again she was being directed by her father in knowing that if the Duke was threatened, she would be able to protect him.

"I love you! I love you!" she was saying over and over again.

They entered the building where the Submarine Cable ended its long journey from the India Office in London.

There were two sentries on duty outside, and inside there was an ordinary office room with three men seated at wooden desks.

The Morse Code messages came from a strange-looking machine that seemed comparatively unimportant for the work it had to do.

"This is what you wished to see, My Lord," the Official said as they entered, "and I must admit, I find it one of the wonders of the age!"

"I agree with you," the Duke replied. "How is it possible that the British could have thought of anything so fantastic that a message sent from London can be here in a few hours."

He laughed and added:

"We have taken nearly nineteen days to arrive!"

"I dare say Your Lordship is aware," the Official said, "that it costs four shillings to send a cable in England at the standard rate to us in India! It is a pity that as human beings we cannot travel by Morse!"

Everyone laughed at his joke.

They moved nearer to the men who were taking down the coded messages.

Solita, however, instead of looking at the machine, was looking at the three Indians who were working it.

Automatically, she began praying that she could be perceptive about them.

She sent out her vibrations towards them.

One of the men's skin was a little darker than the others and she guessed he came from the North.

He looked up as she was watching him.

She thought, although it might have been just her imagination, there was something hard, perhaps hostile in his eyes as he looked at the Duke.

Then suddenly, as if a voice told her what to do, she said loudly in Russian:

"Look out! There is a snake just behind you!"

At the sound of her voice the three Englishmen turned slowly to look at her and two of the Indians did the same.

Only the man she was watching jumped up from his seat and turned round hastily.

Then she pointed her left hand at him accusingly, saying:

"There is your spy!"

For a moment no one moved, then the Indian who was standing pulled a revolver from the pocket of his trousers.

"Stand back!" he said to the Duke, who was nearest to him. "If you come near me I will kill you!"

As he spoke, with his revolver pointing at the Duke's heart, he began backing towards the door.

It was then that Solita, whose right hand was already in her pocket, shot him through the arm.

The bullet passed through her muslin skirt, and the explosion seemed to echo deafeningly round the room.

The Indian dropped his revolver and clasped his other hand to his injured arm before he collapsed to the floor.

As he did so the other two Indians rushed to his side.

The door opened and the sentries who had been on duty outside came in.

As soon as they appeared, the Duke went to Solita and putting his arm around her took her from the room.

They went out onto the compound, and only when they were away from the building did he say:

"You have saved me for the third time, my precious. Could anyone be more clever?"

"I . . . I felt as if there was a voice, perhaps it was Papa's, telling me . . . what to . . . do," Solita faltered.

"Can you walk as far as the House?" the Duke enquired.

"I . . . I am . . . all right."

The Duke was aware, however, that she sounded a little shaky.

At that moment an empty rickshaw was passing them and he shouted at the driver, drawing it to stop, and lifted Solita into it.

As he did so Willy came up to them.

"That was brilliant!" he said to Solita.

She did not answer. She merely shut her eyes for a moment as she said a prayer of thankfulness.

The Duke was safe—for the moment.

They had no idea whether the Russians in India would have been told by the Princess that they had gone to France.

Perhaps she was already aware that his destination was Calcutta.

"Thank You . . . Thank You . . . God . . . for helping me," Solita prayed. "At the same time . . . he is still . . . in danger."

She opened her eyes to find that they were at the house and the Duke was lifting her out of the rickshaw.

He gave her his arm to help her up the steps.

Only when they reached the hall did she say:

"I . . . I think I would . . . like to . . . lie down."

The Duke picked her up in his arms.

"Show me the way to the Memsahib's bedroom," he said to a servant.

They walked for a long way down a high passage to where the bedrooms were situated.

Solita's room was very large and cool with windows opening onto the garden.

The Duke set her down on the bed and when she had taken off her hat he laid her back against the pillows.

"You were marvellous, my darling!" he said. "And once again I owe my life to you."

He glanced over his shoulder and saw there was nobody else in the room.

He could hear Willy's voice giving orders to the servants outside.

He wanted desperately to kiss Solita, but knew it would be a mistake.

Instead, he lifted her hand and kissed first the back of it, then, turning it over, the palm, passionately and insistently.

She felt a little thrill go through her which revived her far quicker than anything else could have done.

"I love . . . you," she whispered.

"I worship and adore you!" he answered beneath his breath.

Willy joined them.

"How can you shoot so brilliantly?" he asked in a low voice. "I was wondering what I could do, and cursing Hugo for not allowing me to carry a weapon."

"It was foolish of me," the Duke admitted, "but I had no idea how we could find the traitor, or that he was ready to defend himself with a pistol."

"I will tell you one thing," Willy said. "It is the last time I go anywhere in this country without a revolver."

"It is not the Indians we are afraid of," the Duke reminded him quietly.

Just for a moment both men were silent. Then Willy said:

"All I can say is thank God Solita had more sense than we did!"

He smiled at her as he asked:

"I am still curious to know what you said which made the fellow reveal himself."

Solita gave a weak little chuckle.

"I said: 'There is a snake behind you!'"

Willy put back his head and laughed.

"No wonder he was frightened, and it was absolutely brilliant of you to think of it!"

Solita looked at the Duke.

He understood that she did not wish to tell Willy that she felt as if the idea had come directly from her father.

"What I must do now is to go and tell the Viceroy what has occurred," he said, "and impress upon him that the whole thing must be hushed up."

"Yes, of course," Willy agreed, "and we should also go and see the Officer in charge of guarding the place

and inform him that the injured man is a spy, and a very
dangerous one!"

"You can do that," the Duke said.

"What . . . will happen . . . to him?" Solita asked.

"You are not to worry your head about that," the
Duke said quietly. "Just rest and I will come back to see
you after I have talked to the Viceroy."

He smiled at her.

Then he and Willy left her, closing the door behind
them.

"Thank You . . . God, thank . . . You," Solita was
praying again, "and please . . . help us with . . . the Princess."

*　　*　　*

It was an hour later that the Duke returned.

He came into the room quietly in case she was asleep
and found that she had undressed and got into bed.

It was too hot to need anything more than a sheet
over her.

He stood for a moment, thinking how lovely she
looked with her golden hair falling over her shoulders
and her bare arms resting on the sheet.

"You are back!" Solita exclaimed with a lift in her
voice.

"I am back," the Duke said, "and I have something
to suggest to you, my darling."

He sat down on the side of the bed and took one of
her hands in both of his.

"Was the Viceroy . . . pleased?" she asked.

"He is exceedingly grateful to you, and will thank
you later this evening."

"That will be . . . embarrassing," Solita said, "and I
. . . do not want to talk . . . about it."

"What I want to talk about," the Duke said, "is something very different."

Solita looked at him a little apprehensively, and he said:

"Because I love you, and because I think you love me, I have asked the Viceroy if we can be married very quietly here in his Private Chapel."

For a moment Solita stared at him.

Then her eyes lit up as if they were filled with stars.

"Married?" she murmured. "Did you say...?"

"If I have to die," the Duke said quietly, "then at least it will be knowing you are protected and looked after, and perhaps I will be able to leave behind a son to take my place."

Solita gave a cry half of rapture and half of fear.

"You must...not talk like that...but if I could... marry you it is...everything I could ever...want... and as I have told you already...it would be like...entering the...gates of Heaven!"

"That is what I hoped you would say," the Duke said. "We are therefore being married very quietly and secretly after dinner this evening."

He looked at her for a long moment before he went on:

"There will be nobody at the Service except Willy and the English Parson, who will be sworn to secrecy."

He smiled before he added:

"The Viceroy is a Catholic, and he avers that there is no safer place in the whole of India than his own Private Chapel."

"And...and I will be...your wife!" Solita said softly.

The Duke bent forward and kissed her lips.

It was a very tender kiss, and she felt as if the angels

were singing and she knew she had never felt so happy.

The Duke rose to his feet.

"I am going now, my dearest one, to talk to the Parson, who has been sent for."

His voice deepened as he added:

"Then you will be mine!"

When Solita was dressed for dinner, wearing her best and prettiest gown, she wondered if the Duke would be disappointed that she would not look like a bride.

Her gown was white, but she had no veil and no wreath.

Then she told herself that it would not matter if she wore rags so long as she could be married to the man she loved.

She looked so happy as the Duke escorted her into the huge Drawing Room where the guests were assembling before dinner that everybody stared.

She was not only beautiful but radiant with happiness.

The *Aides-de-Camp* introduced them to the other guests, some of whom were English, and some Indian.

They all stood in a long line as the Viceroy and Vicereine came into the room.

They shook hands with everybody present, the men bowing, the ladies curtseying because the Viceroy represented the Monarch.

They proceeded into dinner, and it was a pageant of beauty and luxury.

All Solita could think about was that in a few hours she would be married to the Duke.

She knew he was thinking the same thing.

As their eyes met their love seemed to fly one to the other like white doves.

At last the dinner was over and as was usual in India

the guests immediately began to leave, so there was no need for the Duke and Solita to slip away.

They said goodnight to a few people who were left, and with her heart thumping with excitement Solita looked at the Duke.

"Before we go to the Chapel, there is something waiting for you in your bedroom," he said.

She asked no questions, she only walked with him down the passage which led to her bedroom.

As she opened the door she realised it was different from how she had left it.

Now there were many more flowers to grace the room, and on the chaise longue at the foot of the bed there was a large cardboard box.

The Duke undid the string and took off the lid.

Solita looked inside and gave a little cry of delight. It was what she had wanted.

She drew out an exquisite Brussels lace veil.

The Duke took it from her and arranged it over her head, but not over her face.

Beneath it in the box was a leather case which contained, as Solita anticipated, a diamond tiara.

"The Vicereine was very sympathetic," the Duke said, "and she understood that today, of all days, you would want it to be one to remember."

The Duke arranged the tiara on her head, then he kissed her very tenderly and gently.

"The next time I kiss you," he said, "you will be my wife!"

As he finished speaking there was a knock on the door and Willy came in.

"Everything is ready," he announced, "the Chapel is not far from here, so you will not be seen."

Solita took the Duke's arm and they walked down the

empty passages until they came to the small Chapel. It had been specially arranged in Government House for the Viceroy.

The altar was ablaze with candles and there were large ones in carved gold stands on either side of it.

There were white flowers on the altar and large vases of lilies on the steps.

The Parson was waiting.

As Solita walked towards him on the Duke's arm, she felt sure her father and mother were near her.

She had found love as they had done.

The Service did not take long, and the Duke made his vows in a deep, serious voice.

Solita knew he was pledging himself not only to her, but also to God for the rest of his life.

"How could any man be more wonderful?" she asked.

She knew as she received the blessing that she had indeed been blessed and she must be worthy of him.

Then they were walking back alone while Willy had disappeared.

They went into her bedroom and the fragrance of the flowers filled the air.

The lights were very low and outside Solita knew the stars were filling the sky.

Then the Duke's arms were around her and he said in a voice that seemed part of the blessing they had both received:

"You are mine! My wife! And I will love you through all eternity!"

* * *

The Viceroy's Private Train carried the Duke and Duchess of Calverleigh away from Calcutta.

As Willy had said teasingly as they said goodbye, they looked very "posh."

It was an extremely impressive train in white, red, and gold, and very comfortable.

There seemed to Solita an army of servants to look after them.

They were going to Simla, where the Viceroy had lent them his house, "Peterhof," for their honeymoon.

High up in the hills among the trees and brilliant rhododendron bushes, it received the cool air from the mountains around it.

The Duke knew there would be no place in the whole of India so ideal, and where, if they did not wish it, no one would disturb them.

He was desperate to have Solita to himself.

Although he tried not to think of it, he felt that every moment they could be together was infinitely precious.

He was afraid the Russian menace might be nearer to them than they suspected.

To Solita the train was a magic chariot carrying them away.

It did not matter where, so long as she was alone with the Duke to tell her of his love.

Because he was so experienced, he knew because she was so young and innocent that he must be very controlled and very gentle.

Their marriage had been so different from what either of them might have expected.

The Duke was alive when he might by now be dead or injured.

As they both thought of it, they were swept into a rapture that was indescribable.

They were in the Heaven where Solita believed the Duke had taken her.

He had known that never in his long experience had he felt the ecstasy that Solita gave him.

There was also a reverence for her because she filled a shrine within his heart that had until now been empty.

He could only pray as he had never prayed before in the whole of his life that he would be worthy of her.

They talked together during the day.

Later in the bed that seemed to fill the whole carriage nothing could have been more perfect.

They were safe in the train, guarded at every station by soldiers travelling with them, and attendants who were completely loyal to the English.

There was so much to look at through the windows, but the Duke found it hard to take his eyes off Solita.

She grew more beautiful every day as she responded to his love.

It seemed to make her shine as if there were a hidden light inside her.

"I love you! I love you!"

They seemed to say the same words over and over again, and yet they were always new.

Just before they reached Simla, Solita gave a little sigh.

"I wish we could travel on this train for ever and ever!" she said.

"That is how I would feel if I did not know that we shall be just as happy and alone in Peterhof," the Duke replied.

Solita would have thought it was a funny name if she had not felt her heart beating excitedly because she and the Duke would still be together.

No one need come near them unless they wanted them.

It was only then, for the first time, she asked the frightening question.

They were lying in the huge, comfortable bed in a room decked with flowers and the moon and stars were shining outside the windows.

"How long . . . will our . . . honeymoon . . . last?"

"Until we are ready to return to the world in which we both have a part to play," the Duke replied.

"I feel I shall . . . never be . . . ready to do . . . that!"

"That is how I feel too," the Duke said, "but, my darling, some day we must be brave enough to go back. But for the moment I want only to make love to you. I feel as if we have reached the very edge of the world."

Solita put out her arms to draw his head down to hers.

"How could . . . anything be more . . . enchanting?" she asked. "And if this is a dream . . . I never . . . want to . . . wake up!"

"I will make sure you never do," the Duke said. "As long as we are together, my darling, the magic will always be there."

She felt a little throb of fear.

Then, because he was kissing her, it was impossible to think of anything else but him.

They were no longer two people, but one.

* * *

As they sat on the balcony having breakfast, the Duke said:

"Do you realise, my darling, that we have been here a week today?"

"It has . . . gone by too . . . quickly!" Solita replied despairingly.

The Duke laughed.

"That is the sort of compliment I want to hear, even at breakfast."

"We do not have to leave yet?" Solita asked.

He shook his head.

"I plan to stay for at least another seven hundred years! Or in modern parlance—seven days!"

Solita tried to smile at him, but the fear was back in her heart like a heavy stone.

They were interrupted by a servant bringing them in the mail, which had just arrived.

There was a letter for the Duke and *The Times* news-paper.

He set the letter down on the table but Solita did not wish to read it.

England seemed a very long way away.

She did not want to think of what might be happen-ing in London or at the Castle.

The letter which the Duke was opening looked very impressive and Solita realised it was from the Viceroy.

She must have looked anxious, for the Duke smiled at her before he opened it.

He read it, then in a strange voice he said:

"I want you to listen to this, my darling!"

"What . . . is it?" Solita enquired nervously.

"The Viceroy writes to me in his own hand," the Duke began.

My dear Hugo,
I have just received "The Times" from England, and hasten to send it to you as quickly as possible by special train. I am sure you will feel as relieved as I do at the news and we can only both thank God that episode is finished.
After you left, I made sure that any cables men-

*tioning what had occurred were destroyed so that
there could be nothing in the Indian newspapers. The
first anyone will know of it in this country, will be
what they read in "The Times." My wife and I send
you and your wife our best wishes and once again
congratulations on what from the British point of
view is a great victory!*

I remain,

Your affectionate cousin,

Ripon

The Duke finished reading, and Solita, who had been
holding her breath, asked:

"What has happened? What has occurred? Look
quickly . . . !"

Because her tone was urgent, the Duke tore the
wrapping off *The Times* and opening the pages saw his
name on the centre page. He then read:

TRAGEDY AT DUCAL CASTLE

A Joke which turned into a Disaster . . .

Solita once again held her breath as the Duke read
aloud:

*Princess Zenka Kozlovski and Prince Ivan Vlasov,
guests of the Duke of Calverleigh, wished to play a
joke on him. He was away from home convalescing
in France from the recurrence of a fever he had ac-
quired in the East.*

The Princess and her brother, however, thought when he returned to find his family jewels were missing he would be upset until they told him it was only a trick.

They therefore dressed up in masks and burglar-like clothes and crept down to the safe long after midnight. They had the safe open when they were surprised by the Duke's nightwatchmen who are retired soldiers, specially picked for their task.

The Prince apparently drew out his revolver as the soldiers approached him and his sister, and threatened to shoot the men if they came any nearer.

In self-defence, thinking the two Russians were criminals, the nightwatchmen shot them both. Prince Ivan died immediately and his sister two hours later, when the doctors failed to save her.

It was a tragic end to what is believed to be a close friendship between the Duke of Calverleigh and Princess Zenka Kozlovski, who was a well-known Beauty.

Both Russians were buried in the Russian Cemetery in London and the wreaths from their many English friends were impressive.

The Duke of Calverleigh was informed of the tragedy but was not well enough to return from France to attend the Funerals.

The Duke finished reading and gave a deep sigh.

"I cannot believe it!" he said after a moment.

"You said, darling, that the gods were . . . working with . . . us," Solita murmured.

She got up as she spoke and walked to the Duke's side.

For a moment he just looked up at her, then he rose to take her in his arms.

"How can we be so incredibly lucky?" he asked.

"And now we are safe ... safe for ever and we need no longer be afraid!" Solita murmured.

There was a rapture in her voice, then she said a little hesitatingly.

"Y-you do not ... think?"

"I know what you are going to ask," the Duke said, "but it will be impossible for the Secret Police to have any suspicions, or for the Princess to have connected with them. Look at the date. It was the Tuesday after we left."

"Of course! I see that now!" Solita exclaimed. "And the Princess still believed that you were in France, and ... loving her."

Solita's voice faltered on the last two words.

"I never loved her!" the Duke said passionately. "And that, I swear before God, is true. I desired her, but that is a different thing."

He pulled her against him.

"The love I have for you, my darling, is part of God, and comes from the stars. That is real love, the love I have sought all my life and thought I would never find."

"Oh, darling Hugo, that is ... what I wanted ... you to ... say," Solita murmured.

"I will say it now, and I will go on saying it," the Duke replied, "but I will not say it in words, I will say it more positively when you are closer to me than you are now."

She looked up at him, her lips ready for his.

Her eyes were shining and filled with the sunshine that was just coming through the clouds.

The Duke looked at her for a long moment.

"I adore you," he said in his deep voice, "and there is only one way I can tell you how much."

He picked her up in his arms and carried her back into their bedroom.

He laid her down on the bed, then as he joined her he knew that his heart was singing and that, as Solita had said, the gods had been with them, and they had won.

"Darling . . . darling . . . I am so happy!" Solita whispered. "How could anything be more wonderful than that you are safe, and need no longer be . . . afraid!"

"I am safe with you, as you are safe with me!" the Duke said.

"There is only one thing that still worries me."

"What is that?" he asked.

As he spoke, his lips were moving over the softness of her skin and his hand was touching her body.

"It is," Solita said in a very small voice, "that you . . . might find it . . . boring . . . just to be with me . . . and not be taking part in as many of those . . . dangerous missions . . . as you have done in the past."

The Duke looked down at her.

"There are other ways of serving our country," he said, "and those we will do together because I now belong to you, and to the children we shall have in the future. I will never again challenge the Russians, nor, if I can help it, become involved with any of them again!"

Solita gave a little cry of happiness.

"That is what I . . . wanted you to . . . say. Oh, Hugo, I love you so much! Please show me how to . . . fill your life so that it is . . . complete without . . . danger."

"It is complete with you!" the Duke said firmly.

Then he was kissing her fiercely, passionately, possessively, and she knew that it was his relief from the fear that had been inside them, and which they were both afraid to acknowledge.

"I love you! I love you!" Solita said. "Oh, Hugo . . . love me, my darling, and teach me . . . how to make you . . . happy!"

"I am happy at this moment," the Duke said, "so happy that I feel as if we have reached the top of the Himalayas. We have conquered the world, and are now in the Heaven to which you told me we belong."

"We are . . . together."

Then there was no need for words.

They were, as the Duke had said, in a Heaven where there was only sunshine and happiness, and no evil or fear could encroach.

They were blessed by God, who would protect them from now until Eternity.

ABOUT THE AUTHOR

Barbara Cartland, the world's most famous romantic novelist, who is also an historian, playwright, lecturer, political speaker and television personality, has now written over 500 books and sold nearly 500 million copies all the world over.

She has also had many historical works published and has written four autobiographies as well as the biographies of her mother and that of her brother, Ronald Cartland, who was the first Member of Parliament to be killed in the last war. This book has a preface by Sir Winston Churchill and has just been republished with an introduction by the late Sir Arthur Bryant.

Love at the Helm, a novel written with the help and inspiration of the late Earl Mountbatten of Burma, Great Uncle of His Royal Highness The Prince of Wales, is being sold for the Mountbatten Memorial Trust.

She has broken the world record for the last thirteen years by writing an average of twenty-three books a year. In the Guiness Book of Records she is listed as the world's top-selling author.

Miss Cartland in 1978 sang an Album of Love Songs with the Royal Philharmonic Orchestra.

In private life Barbara Cartland, who is a Dame of the Order of St. John of Jerusalem, Chairman of the St. John Council in Hertfordshire and Deputy

President of the St. John Ambulance Brigade, has fought for better conditions and salaries for Midwives and Nurses.

She championed the cause for the Elderly in 1956 invoking a Government Enquiry into the "Housing Conditions of Old People."

In 1962 she had the Law of England changed so that Local Authorities had to provide camps for their own Gypsies. This has meant that since then thousands and thousands of Gypsy children have been able to go to School, which they had never been able to do in the past, as their caravans were moved every twenty-four hours by the Police.

There are now fourteen camps in Hertfordshire and Barbara Cartland has her own Romany Gypsy Camp called Barbaraville by the Gypsies.

Her designs "Decorating with Love" are being sold all over the U.S.A. and the National Home Fashions League made her, in 1981, "Woman of Achievement."

She is unique in that she was one and two in the Dalton list of Best Sellers, and one week had four books in the top twenty.

Barbara Cartland's book *Getting Older, Growing Younger* has been published in Great Britain and the U.S.A. and her fifth cookery Book, *The Romance of Food*, is now being used by the House of Commons.

In 1984 she received at Kennedy Airport America's Bishop Wright Air Industry Award for her contribution to the development of aviation. In 1931 she and two R.A.F. Officers thought of, and carried, the first aeroplane-towed glider airmail.

During the War she was Chief Lady Welfare

Officer in Bedfordshire looking after 20,000 Service men and women. She thought of having a pool of Wedding Dresses at the War Office so a Service Bride could hire a gown for the day.

She bought 1,000 gowns without coupons for the A.T.S., the W.A.A.F.'s and the W.R.E.N.S. In 1945 Barbara Cartland received the Certificate of Merit from Eastern Command.

In 1964 Barbara Cartland founded the National Association for Health of which she is the President, as a front for all the Health Stores and for any product made as alternative medicine.

This is now a £300,000 turnover a year, with one third going in export.

In January 1988 she received "La Médaille de Vermeil de la Ville de Paris." This is the highest award to be given in France by the City of Paris for achievement. She has sold 25 million of her books in France.